Nancy Drew
in
The Mystery of the Tolling Bell

The Nancy Drew Mystery Stories

The Mystery of the Tolling Bell

Carolyn Keene

Armada

First published in the U.K. in 1972 by
William Collins Sons & Co. Ltd., London and Glasgow.
First published in Armada in 1979 by
Fontana Paperbacks,
14 St. James's Place, London SW1A 1PS.

This impression 1982.

Printed in Great Britain by
Love & Malcomson Ltd., Brighton Road,
Redhill, Surrey.

The cover picture shows Pamela Sue Martin as Nancy Drew
in the MCA television production of Nancy Drew.

CONTENTS

·1· *An Unusual Pushcart*

"NANCY, aren't we almost at Candleton? I'm tired of driving."

A freckled, athletic-looking girl, with the boyish name of George Fayne, stretched wearily in the roadster which sped along towards the ocean.

Nancy Drew, who was driving, shrugged her shoulders and breathed deeply of the tangy salt air. A gust of wind blew her golden hair across her eyes. Tossing it aside, she smiled at the two girls with her; George, and George's cousin, Bess Marvin.

"A few more miles," she replied. "But it's worth waiting for."

"You mean because of the mystery at Candleton?" Bess asked teasingly. "Personally, right now I'm more interested in food and getting myself fixed up."

Opening a compact, she gazed in its mirror at her shiny snub nose. Forgetting for a moment that the mirror magnified, she wrinkled her forehead in displeasure and added:

"Maybe I ought to diet!"

Nancy laughed. "We have to eat, figure or no figure," she said. "Perhaps we'll come to a fishing village where we can get some lobster. Like it?"

"Never ate any," replied Bess, who preferred cake and ice cream to any other kind of food.

The three girls, who lived in River Heights, were en route to Candleton on White Cap Bay. They had been invited to spend a brief vacation there as the guests of

7

Mrs John Chantrey. For many years Mrs Chantrey had been a close friend and client of Nancy's father, the well-known lawyer, Carson Drew. He was to meet the girls in the little town.

"I think your father was smart to make the trip by plane instead of riding with us," George observed as the car swung round another sharp curve. "At least he won't die of starvation."

"This is really a business trip for Dad," Nancy said, to divert the minds of her friends from food. "Poor Mrs Chantrey was swindled out of a lot of money, and Dad is trying to get it back for her."

"How did she lose it?" George asked curiously.

"Dad didn't tell me many of the details," Nancy replied. "But he did hint at mystery, and said I might help him. Mrs Chantrey is a lovely person, and I hope we can help her. She was once very wealthy, you know."

"Now she runs a tearoom?" George inquired.

"Yes. She decided to open a gift shop and tearoom after she lost most of her money."

"I was hoping the mystery at Candleton would be about something more romantic than just lost money," remarked Bess in disappointment.

Nancy's eyes twinkled. "Oh, but there is another mystery!" she said. "Maybe you'll like that one better. Mrs Chantrey mentioned in her letter that something ghostly and unexplainable happens along the coast of White Cap Bay."

"Well, that's different," said George, interested at once. "Is your father going to work on that, too?"

"Oh, no," Nancy laughed. "He's a lawyer, not a detective! His only interest in Candleton is to get back Mrs Chantrey's money."

"Nancy, you know that your father is the best lawyer

in the state! He could solve any problem," Bess declared confidently.

"He also has an equally clever daughter named Nancy," added George loyally. "Furthermore, she has two able helpers! If the three of us can't solve the two mysteries of White Cap Bay in next to no time —"

"Look!" Bess interrupted, pointing to a sign on the right-hand side of the road. "Fisher's Cove!" she fairly shouted. "We're coming to a town!"

Driving on to Main Street, they saw two hotels and several restaurants. Nancy noticed a sign with the name Wayside Inn. An arrow under the sign pointed up a side road.

"Let's go there," she suggested. "It sounds attractive."

She turned the car and presently they came to a freshly painted, white house overlooking the surf.

"This is fine!" George approved. "Pull up under that tree, Nancy."

The Wayside Inn proved to be cool, clean and inviting. Although the hour was late, the woman in charge assured the girls she could serve them luncheon.

"We have only puffed shrimp and French fried clams left," she announced.

Nancy found her luncheon very appetizing. In addition to the sea food there were tomatoes, cabbage salad, potatoes, lemonade, and for dessert, apple pie.

"I know I've gained a dozen pounds!" Bess moaned as they paid their bill and left the inn. "I shouldn't have eaten so much."

"I feel like a puffed shrimp myself!" groaned George. "Let's walk round Fisher's Cove awhile before we drive on. A little exercise will be good for us."

Although eager to reach Candleton, Nancy agreed to the suggestion. Leaving the car under the tree, they took a path which led from the sandy shore to the main street of the village.

"Oh, look!" cried Nancy suddenly, as she came to a corner. "Isn't that attractive?"

From a side street came the musical tinkle of a bell. At first Bess and George, some distance behind her, saw nothing. But a moment later a dark-haired woman pushing a flower-decked cart came into view. Spying the girls, she moved briskly towards them.

"Wonder what she's selling," Bess said in an undertone.

From a wire stretched across the cart dangled strings of tiny red metal hearts and a little bell.

The woman, obviously of foreign birth, wore a long red and white costume with an embroidered red heart on one sleeve. As she drew near to the girls, she addressed them in a torrent of words.

"You buy from Madame? I sell all zese articles *tres bon* for beautyment. Come see." She held up a bottle of perfume, some powder, and a lipstick.

By this time quite a number of people had gathered about the cart. Many in the crowd were young country girls who seemed awed by the elaborate display of cosmetics.

"Just like ze city girls buy in New York," Madame glorified her products. "Sold only in ze best salons."

"I don't recall seeing that brand before," Nancy remarked, observing that all the cosmetic containers bore the French words *Mon Coeur*.

"It means 'my heart'," translated Madame. "Powder, lipstick, rouge, and perfume, zey come in sets. Zey bring to mademoiselle beauty and allure."

"How much?" inquired a rather unattractive, large-boned country girl.

"For ze perfume, three dollars. One lipstick, rouge for ze cheeks, powder, and ze smallest heart of perfume —you take all, I make it five dollars."

"That's a lot of money," commented the country girl.

"I give you demonstration to go wiz ect."

"All right."

Madame took the note offered her, then quickly applied the cosmetics to the girl's face. The woman's sales talk convinced other bystanders. They bought the *Mon Coeur* products freely, while the blonde country girl walked to a mirrored showcase window in a shop to admire herself. To the horror of Nancy and George, she promptly put on more of the cosmetics and sprinkled herself liberally with the perfume. Then, satisfied but conspicuous, she went down the street.

Bess had been watching Madame steadily, and could not resist the temptation to buy. "I'll take a small bottle of perfume," she decided. "Also this lipstick and powder."

"Bess!" remonstrated George. "You don't know a thing about *Mon Coeur* products!"

"My zings are of ze finest," Madame retorted angrily. "You have no right—"

"Bess, do come away," Nancy urged her friend.

Bess might have retreated without buying, but quick as a flash Madame thrust the articles into her hand and snatched the money the girl had taken from her purse.

"Is this perfume the same as in the sample bottle?" Bess asked doubtfully, observing that the contents of the vial were lighter in colour than the liquid in the opened bottle.

"Zey all ze same," snapped the woman. Giving Bess the change, she started hurriedly down the street with the flower-decked pushcart.

In her haste to get away, Madame cut directly across the road. The little bell jangled and the heart-shaped decorations swung back and forth.

A trap and old white horse came jogging down the street, its driver drowsing at the reins. Suddenly something frightened the mare. It gave a startled snort. Before the elderly driver realized what was happening, the animal bolted straight towards the woman and her cart.

With a scream of terror, Madame abandoned her cosmetics and raced for safety, dodging into a shop. The horse plunged wildly along the street, pulling the trap over the kerb, then back into the street again. Nearly all the pedestrians had taken cover, for no one could guess which way the frightened animal would gallop next.

The flower-decked cart stood deserted in the middle of the street, directly in the path of the runaway horse. Before Bess or George could stop her, Nancy darted out and wheeled the cart to safety. A moment later the horse flashed by. Not until they had gone another block did the driver of the trap finally recover control of his mare.

"Nancy, you might have been killed!" Bess cried out. She was trembling.

"I agree with you," Nancy replied, parking the cart under an awning. "I acted impulsively. Well, shall we get the car and go on to Candleton?"

"The sooner we get there, the better I'll like it," agreed Bess.

Without waiting for Madame to return, the three friends started to cross the street. As Nancy stepped down from the kerb a poorly dressed woman rushed up to her and seized her arm.

"You're the one!" she screamed. "I'm going to have you arrested!"

Startled, Nancy retreated a step. But the excited woman pursued her, holding tightly on to her arm.

"You're a thief, and you've got no business in this town!" she shouted in a hoarse voice. "You've ruined my daughter and taken her money! Police! Police!"

· 2 ·   A Strange Customer

NANCY pulled herself free from the excited woman. By this time Bess and George, aware that their friend was in difficulty, darted to Nancy's side.

"Police! Police!" the woman screamed again. "My daughter's been robbed!"

"Who is your daughter?" Nancy asked the woman sharply.

"You should know! You sold her that there red stuff she put on her cheeks and lips!"

Light dawned upon Nancy. "Then your daughter is the girl who bought several things from Madame with the pushcart."

"She bought them from you!" the woman accused the Drew girl. "Oh, you needn't look so innocent! I saw you wheel that cart o' yours out of the street when that horse ran away!"

Nancy explained that Madame sold the cosmetics, not she. Bess and George supported her story, but the farm woman would not listen.

"Here comes a policeman now!" George muttered in Nancy's ear.

It was not the first time Nancy Drew had found herself in a predicament. Her young life had been fairly crammed with adventure.

Nancy's mother was dead. For many years the girl had been reared by Mrs Gruen, the family housekeeper, whom she regarded almost as a parent. Because Nancy was unusually sensible, clever and talented, Mrs Gruen allowed her a great deal of freedom, particularly when she was assisting her father on one of his cases.

Nevertheless, the housekeeper sometimes felt that Nancy took entirely too many risks. She had not approved when only a few months earlier those inseparable companions, Bess, George and Nancy, had explored Heath Castle, an abandoned estate not far from the city of River Heights. Their investigations had resulted in finding the "Clue in the Crumbling Wall," but Nancy had spent many trying hours locked in an ancient dungeon before the adventure was over.

Now, as the policeman ran towards the girls, Nancy waited calmly, for she knew she had done nothing wrong.

"What's going on here?" the patrolman demanded as he hurried up to the group.

"This girl robbed me!" the woman accused. " She tricked my daughter into buying a lot of trash to put on her face."

"This woman has mistaken me for someone else," Nancy said quietly.

"Then where is the other person?" demanded Nancy's accuser.

The girls turned to gaze towards the spot where they had left the cart. It was gone! Madame must have taken it away.

"I want my money back!" the woman resumed her tirade.

"See here," said the policeman sternly, "you're creating an unnecessary disturbance. What is your charge against this girl?"

"That she sold my daugher a lot of worthless rubbish!"

At this moment a man stepped up to the group, introduced himself as Professor Atkins, and said he had seen the whole episode from down the street. Smiling at Nancy, he told how she had saved the flower-decked pushcart and had not received so much as a thank-you from its owner. The woman turned pale.

"I—I guess I've made a mistake," she muttered. "Forget what I said."

She retreated hastily. Nancy thanked the professor. Then, eager to leave, she quickly led the way to her car and drove out of town.

En route to Candleton, Bess opened the vial of *Mon Coeur* perfume she had bought. After she had sniffed the perfume, the girl gazed at her companions a bit sheepishly.

"I'm afraid I was swindled," she said. "This isn't as good as the sample."

"It's fragrant, anyway," Nancy remarked soothingly, as Bess held the bottle under her friend's nose.

Then George sniffed at the bottle and pretended to collapse on the cushions. "This would slay a man instead of making him propose, as Madame suggested. Take my advice and throw it away."

"And waste all my money?" Bess recorked the bottle. "No. I'll keep it."

The road no longer offered the monotonous scenery it had on the other side of Fisher's Cove. Instead, it ran lazily along moors carpeted with low-growing juniper, and at points the rocks split into colourful masses over which leaped the sea's filmy spray.

"We're not far from Candleton now," Nancy declared, as cliffs loomed in the distance.

Abruptly the car rounded a bend, and the girls caught their first glimpse of White Cap Bay. Never before had they seen such a stretch of beautiful water. Once only a fishing town, the little village of Candleton was now a fashionable summer resort with attractive cottages and fine hotels.

Mrs Chantrey's comfortable home stood at some distance from the beach, just beyond the business section of the town. Nancy drove the car up an attractive private drive and stopped in front of the house.

A young Negro maid opened the door, and smilingly said that she was Juno. She helped them carry their luggage to their rooms, and explained that her mistress was at the tearoom. Mrs Chantrey had left word that the girls were to make themselves at home.

"Let's go down to the tearoom," George suggested.

Presently the girls saw Mrs Chantrey's tearoom, the Salsandee Shop. Bright-coloured umbrellas dotted its outdoor dining-room and garden.

"What a clever name," Bess observed, as Nancy explained the tearoom specialized in salads and sandwiches. "What does the 'dee' stand for?"

"I don't know. We'll have to ask Mrs Chantrey."

A number of customers were seated in the outdoor dining-room waiting to be served, while others were waiting inside. A harassed waitress moved swiftly about, trying without success to take a dozen orders. Nervous and confused, she showed her annoyance as Nancy stopped her to inquire for Mrs Chantrey.

"She's in the kitchen," the girl replied, "but please don't bother her now unless it's important. Several of our girls failed to show up today, and we're nearly frantic trying to serve everyone."

Nancy and her chums might have gone away quietly to await Mrs Chantrey at her home, had not an idea occurred to Nancy.

"Why don't we pitch in and help her?" she demanded. "We've waited on tables before!"

"It would be fun!" agreed George.

Seeking their hostess in the kitchen, they found her frantically making dozens of salads. Bread in the toaster started to burn. With an exclamation of impatience, she switched off the current.

Mrs Chantrey, a woman in her mid-forties, was ordinarily a serene and attractively groomed person. Now a wisp of grey hair tumbled down over one eye, and a splotch of tomato ketchup stained her apron.

"Hello?" said Nancy cheerfully. "Do you need any help?"

Mrs Chantrey dropped a knife. Her face mirrored dismay. "Why, it's Nancy Drew, and these are your friends!" she gasped. "How ashamed I am to be found in such a state!"

"You need help and we're here to give it," Nancy offered with a smile. "Just tell us what to do."

"I can't put you girls to work the first moment you arrive! Why, you're my guests!"

"We'd like to do it," Bess spoke up. "Please let us."

"Then I won't protest any longer. You're a gift straight from heaven! If you can help out for an hour, the worst of the rush will be over."

Chatting excitedly, Mrs Chantrey tied aprons on the three girls. While George remained in the kitchen to make sandwiches, Nancy and Bess were sent to wait on tables. Seeking Dora, the waitress they had met a few minutes earlier, they requested instructions.

"You take the tables out in the garden," the girl directed Nancy, sizing her up as the more efficient of the two girls. "Bess and I will handle the inside dining-room. Here are your order pads. Don't try to carry too many dishes or you may have an accident."

"Waitress!" called an impatient voice.

"Everyone is in a dreadful mood," Dora whispered. "Some have been waiting nearly an hour for their food."

Nancy moved swiftly among the tables assigned to her. She took orders efficiently, learning the names of the dishes which made the Salsandee Shop so popular. A steady flow of food began to arrive from the kitchen, including the popular three-decker grilled lobster, cheese and tomato sandwich; the mixed green salad with minced ham and clam dressing; and the Dandee Tart, filled with steaming hot fish pudding topped with salmon-coloured meringue. The girls learned that the last syllable of the name Salsandee was derived from the "dee" in Dandee.

Customers, at first impatient and cross, soon began to smile at Nancy. After clearing one place she was amazed to find a dollar tip.

One of the last diners in the garden was a white-haired man with spectacles. He dawdled over a frosted glass of iced tea. Nancy hovered near, hopeful that he would leave, but instead he became talkative.

"Do you live here?" he inquired.

"No, I'm just a visitor, helping out," Nancy explained. "Actually, I'm not a waitress."

"Well, I'm a stranger to this town myself. Came here looking for a bell."

Nancy remained politely silent.

"Not an ordinary bell, but one that was made in a casting furnace in Boston during the Revolutionary War. A Paul Revere bell—that's what I'm after."

"Then you're an antique collector?" Nancy asked, becoming interested.

"Not exactly. Those old bells are valuable as antiques, but I want this particular one for another reason." The old man gazed at her with shrewd eyes. "They tell me there are any number of old bells to be had around this town."

"I wouldn't know about that," Nancy replied. "I arrived here only a few hours ago."

"I see, I see," muttered the stranger. Hurriedly drinking his iced tea, he dropped a coin by his plate and went down the path towards the ocean.

Wondering who the man might be, Nancy began to clear away the dishes. She dropped the coin in her pocket, intending to give it, and the other tips, to Dora.

As the girl picked up a plate, she noticed a folded piece of paper on the floor at her feet and brushed it aside. Then the thought struck her that the paper might be important. Perhaps the diner who had just left the garden dropped it.

Putting down her tray, Nancy picked up the paper. The handwriting on it was very old-fashioned. A puzzled look came over her face as she read the words, which were in French.

"Whoever finds this may become enormously wealthy," she translated in amazement. "In one of my XXX cast bells are embedded many jewels."

The paper had been torn in half, and the remainder of the strange message was missing!

·3· *Legend of the Cave*

As NANCY reread the mysterious words, Bess Marvin approached the table.

"Thank goodness, the last customer has gone!" she exclaimed, pulling off her apron. "Collect any tips, Nancy?"

"Uh-huh," her friend replied, her mind on the strange message.

"You're not listening!" Bess accused. "What is it you're reading, Nancy?"

"A paper I found on the floor after one of my customers left. He was an odd old fellow, Bess, and he told me he came to Candleton to find an antique bell made by Paul Revere!"

Offering the paper to her friend to read, Nancy waited expectantly for her comments.

"Jewels embedded in an XXX cast bell!" Bess translated. "Why, it's another mystery, Nancy!"

"Not so loud," the other warned with a quick glance around. "If the contents of this paper should become known, some dishonest person in Candleton might start buying up all the old bells around here and selling them at a fancy profit."

"What is an XXX bell, Nancy?"

"I don't know, but my guess is the three X's might be the trademark of the maker."

Mrs Chantrey dropped the paper into a desk drawer, instructing Dora to give it to the stranger, should he call. Then, grateful to the girls for helping her, she insisted they stop work and return to her cottage.

20

"I'll go with you," she declared. "Thanks to you most of the work is done. Dora will be able to take care of the few customers who may drop in between now and closing time."

The moon was coming up as the three girls walked along the beach with their hostess. Farther up White Cap Bay they glimpsed a lighthouse, and Mrs Chantrey pointed out Whistling Oyster Cove and Bald Head Cliff, two distinguished landmarks.

"Such picturesque names!" laughed George, stooping to pick up an odd-shaped shell. "Is fishing the chief occupation here, Mrs Chantrey?"

"I'd say the making of salt-water toffee is!" she chuckled. "And chewing it is the main pastime of the summer residents! But seriously, there is one interesting spot you must visit. Mother Mathilda's Candle Shop."

"Did those lovely ones at the Salsandee Shop come from there?" Bess inquired.

"Yes. You may have noticed they're slightly perfumed."

As Bess and George asked various questions about the village and its inhabitants, Nancy remained unusually quiet. She was thinking about her father, and wondering why he had not arrived. She was startled when her hostess suddenly asked:

"When will your father come to Candleton. Nancy? We were expecting him this morning."

"I thought he'd be here when we arrived," she replied. "He telephoned and said he was taking a plane from New York."

"Maybe he's at the house now," suggested Bess.

"I'm sure he's not." Nancy shook her head. "I left word for him to phone me at the tearoom." Her face became troubled. "I wonder if anything went wrong?" she said.

Although Mr Drew was a busy man, and Nancy understood that he might have been delayed by unexpected business, he had never failed to let his daughter know of a change in his plans.

"Now don't worry about your father," Mrs Chantrey said quickly. "He may have decided to come by train. Perhaps there's a telegram at home."

Nancy brightened at the suggestion. When they came to the cottage a few minutes later, however, she realized that the hope was a vain one. There was no message.

To relieve Nancy's mind, Mrs Chantrey telephoned the telegraph office and the airport. There was no word from the lawyer. Nancy decided that she could not allow worry over her father's absence to spoil the evening for Bess and George, so she pretended to dismiss the matter by saying that he surely would arrive the next morning.

"Tomorrow we must explore White Cap Bay," she declared. "Mrs Chantrey, you hinted at a mystery along the shore."

Her hostess smiled. "It concerns the cave at the base of Bald Head Cliff. My advice to you would be to avoid the spot."

"Please tell us why." Nancy moved forward in her chair.

"I've never been there myself," Mrs Chantrey continued, "but townspeople say it's spooky and dangerous. According to the story—"

"Yes?"

Mrs Chantrey laughed nervously. "I'm not sure I should repeat what I've heard," she said. "But then, I've never shared the superstititions of the local people."

By this time the girls were deeply interested, and begged her to tell them the story.

"According to the tale, Bald Head Cave is inhabited by a ghost," Mrs Chantrey revealed reluctantly. "I don't believe in ghosts, but the fact remains that some unhappy accidents have occurred lately in that area. Several persons nearly drowned, and one man did lose his life."

"How do the accidents happen?" Nancy questioned curiously.

"It's said the ghost causes water to rush out of the cave. It engulfs anyone in its path. He tolls a warning bell whenever reckless individuals venture too near his hideout, and if they don't leave at once there's trouble."

"How long has this been going on?" Nancy asked.

"I don't know exactly," Mrs Chantrey replied. "But not for long—at least, nothing of the sort occurred years ago. From what I hear, I judge the cave has always been here, but not the ghost nor the rushing water and the tolling bell."

"Has the cave been explored?" George asked practically.

"A few venturesome men have tried it but learned nothing. Evidently the ghost keeps close watch over his property."

The story excited Nancy's curiosity. She thought about it late into the night. Since she did not believe in ghosts, she concluded there must be some logical explanation for the phenomenon. As Nancy dropped off to sleep, she decided the only way to find out was to go there herself and investigate. Perhaps in the morning—

But in the morning Nancy forgot about exploring the cave, for no word had come from her father. Unable to hide her alarm, she called her home in River Heights.

Hannah Gruen had heard nothing from Mr Drew and she in turn became worried.

A call to the lawyer's office brought no reassurance. Mr Drew's secretary was on vacation, and the girl who was taking her place said she thought he had gone to Candleton.

"And there was no word from New York?"

"None at all."

Discouraged, Nancy thanked her and hung up. She became more and more worried.

"Perhaps he's been in an accident," she told her friends.

"Now do stop worrying, Nancy," Bess said kindly. "If your father had been in an accident, someone in River Heights would have been notified. Doesn't he always carry identification papers?"

"Yes, but—"

"Your father will be along any hour now, so stop building up gory pictures," George cut in. To get Nancy's mind off the matter, she added, "How about Bald Head Cave? Do we explore it this morning?"

"All right," agreed Nancy with forced cheerfulness. "I wonder how we reach the place?"

They learned from Juno that even at low tide the only safe approach to Bald Head was by motorboat. The maid's eyes rolled in fright when she learned the girls intended to go there, and she warned them not to venture near the cave. Nancy assured her they would be careful. She and her friends left the house and rented a sturdy craft from an old fisherman.

Under Nancy's guidance the little boat putt-putted slowly along the shore. Rising above the water, and stretching out for about two miles, were the colourful cliffs which had attracted artists from all parts of the country.

"I see a man up on that cliff with a telescope," George said, scowling. "He's looking at us. I hate people with telescopes. They have an unfair advantage!"

Nancy laughed as she steered nearer shore. "No doubt summer visitors are resented by the all-year inhabitants."

The man disappeared from view as the boat came into the shadow of the cliff.

"Look! The entrance to the cave!" George cried as they reached a secluded indentation about half a mile from the ocean. "It's rather large."

"Let's just look at it from the outside," Bess suggested nervously.

Nancy smiled as she switched off the boat's motor, allowing the craft to drift closer to shore. "We're safe enough so long as we stay in this boat," she declared. "But you know very well, Bess, we couldn't learn a thing without going inside the cave."

Bess, whose gaze had been focused steadily on the cave entrance, suddenly sat up so jerkily that she caused the boat to rock sideways. Glancing at their friend, Nancy and George were astonished to see that her chubby face mirrored terror.

"What is it?" George whispered.

For a moment Bess, badly shaken, could not speak. Then with a trembling hand, she pointed towards the dark mouth of the cavern, and said shakily:

"The ghost! I saw it in its white robe. It—it went back into the cave!"

·4· **Rushing Water**

STARTLED by Bess's words, Nancy and George gazed anxiously towards the cave entrance. They could see nothing but the dark opening framed by rocks and water.

"You must have imagined it, Bess," declared George. "There's no ghost—nothing white."

"Not now, but it was there!"

"What did it look like?" Nancy asked.

"I saw only a white blur. But then, ghosts aren't supposed to have a regular form."

"You probably mistook a sea gull for a ghost," George laughed.

Bess's lips drew into a thin, stubborn line. "It certainly was not a bird," she argued. "But forget it. Even if that cave were inhabited by twenty ghosts, I know I couldn't talk you two out of exploring it!"

Nancy had no intention of venturing farther in a reckless manner. As the boat drifted closer, she studied the entrance to the cave and listened intently.

"Hear any warning bell?" George asked jokingly.

Nancy shook her head. The only sound was the roar of the ocean in the distance.

"What's your plan?" George inquired after a moment.

"The cave is quite wide and if the water is deep enough we can row the boat inside," Nancy replied. From the bottom of the craft she picked up lead and line and began to take soundings at the entranceway.

"The water is nearly two feet deep inside the cave," she announced, measuring the wet section of the line. "Our boat shouldn't go aground."

Using the oars, the girls cautiously rowed through the cave entrance into the dark interior. Nancy, who always carried a flashlight in her bag, swept its beam over the jagged limestone walls.

The passageway in which the girls found themselves had a natural ledge on one side, etched from the rock by erosion. The walls were damp, and the temperature at least twenty degrees lower than it was in the sunny bay.

"It seems like a very ordinary cavern," commented George, relaxing. "No ghost. No bell. No water pouring out."

Nancy manoeuvred the boat to the ledge and fastened the painter securely to a jagged piece of rock.

"What are you going to do?" Bess demanded.

"I want to walk along the ledge for a short distance. This cave may have an inner room. It's too dark to tell from here, and if we take the boat much farther, we may have difficulty getting out."

Bess was reluctant to leave the boat, but when she saw that George intended going with Nancy, she too climbed out on to the ledge.

Walking ahead, Nancy flashed her light over the dark walls. "Hello!" she exclaimed, and her voice echoed weirdly. "Here's something!"

Bess and George moved closer to their friend. Over her shoulder they glimpsed a massive stone man whose half-closed eyes stared straight at them. Startled, Bess stifled a scream of terror.

"It's only a statue carved out of the rock," George scolded her. "Don't be a goose!"

Nancy's flashlight picked out the details of the figure. "My, it's large enough to be a real man!"

"It *is* real," whispered Bess in horror. "Look at his right hand! It's *moving*!"

Nancy started to say "Nonsense!" but the words froze on her lips. The stone man's upraised hand actually was moving! Even as she watched, it dropped to his side, rolled down the carven body, and fell with a splash into the water!

With a shriek of terror, Bess wheeled about and would have fled, but Nancy seized her wrist.

"It's only a piece of the statue chipping off," she reassured her. "For a second I was fooled too."

A moment later they heard a loud splash directly ahead of them. Focusing their eyes upon the spot, they were dismayed to see a dark object rise out of the water.

"That's no rock!" chattered Bess. "It's—it's something alive!"

The slithering creature, its sides glistening like satin, swam to the rocks, and pulled itself to the ledge.

"A seal!" whispered Nancy in relief. "I'll shoo him back into the water."

The seal, however, showed no interest in leaving his rocky perch. Instead, he rotated his head towards the girls, emitting a deafening bark which nearly split their eardrums.

"Do seals bite?" Bess asked nervously.

"I'm sure I don't know," Nancy replied. "The nearest I ever came to one before was at the zoo. This old fellow acts annoyed. He might do anything."

"I'm not going on!" Bess decided suddenly.

With that, she turned and hurried back towards the boat.

George picked up a small rock, intending to hurl it

at the seal. She raised her arm, only to let it fall to her side. So sharply did she draw in her breath that Nancy, who was standing beside her, heard the sound.

"What is it, George? What did you see?"

The seal had not moved. George's gaze was fixed upon a portion of the ledge far back in the cave.

"The ghost!" she whispered tremulously. "I saw it just then—a figure in white!"

Nancy had observed nothing, but George's fear increased her own growing uneasiness. A sixth sense warned her that they faced danger. For the first time since entering the underground passage, she considered turning back.

"Nancy, we'd better run!" George urged, unashamed. "I don't feel too happy about this place myself."

"It's not fair to leave Bess alone in the boat if something should happen," George said in a hushed voice.

"We'll go," Nancy agreed, her words hardly audible.

The two girls walked rapidly along the ledge towards the entrance. They had taken scarcely a dozen steps when a bell began to toll far back in the cave. Loud and full in tone, the pealing held a mournful note as if tolling for departed spirits.

Electrified by the sound, Nancy and George stopped suddenly. The same terrifying thought came to each of them.

"The warning bell Mrs Chantrey told us about!" cried George. "It rings just before water engulfs the cave!"

Nancy seized her by the hand. "Come on!" she urged. "We must get out of here—fast!"

It was too late!

"Listen!" George cried tensely. "That roaring sound—hear it?"

Both girls froze to the spot, for the sound they heard was the mad rush of a great wall of water plunging towards them with the speed of an express train.

"Run!" screamed Nancy. "Run for your life!"

The boat was still some distance away, tied to the jagged rock. Nancy knew what she and George could never reach it before the water struck them. But Bess, who stood on the ledge beside the craft, might escape.

"Get in the boat! Cast off!" Nancy shouted frantically.

It took Bess only a second to realize her great danger. She bent down to loosen the rope. Paralyzed with fright, her fingers became numb and would not unfasten the knot.

The next instant the great curtain of water raced through the cave, sweeping everything before it. Nancy and George, struggling desperately, were engulfed.

Instinctively Bess clung to the painter of the boat. As the water struck her, the rope snapped free of the rock. The craft raced towards the cave entrance.

Bess, holding fast to the rope, was carried face downwards through the torrent.

• 5 •   *Nancy's Predicament*

ALMOST suffocated, Bess clung with all her strength to the rope as the boat shot from the mouth of the cave. Finally, when the speed of the craft lessened, she took a deep breath, and grasped the gunwale.

The motorboat was half-filled with water. Should she climb aboard? No, it probably would sink. Swimming with one hand, the girl tried to tow the boat towards shore. It was difficult going.

Frantically her eyes darted towards the cave entrance. Water still boiled from the cavern's gaping mouth. What had happened to her friends? She could not see them.

"Nancy! George!" she shouted.

There was no answer. Bess did not try to call out again. She concentrated all her efforts upon reaching the rocky beach.

Presently her feet struck bottom. Standing upright, she pulled the boat in so that it could not float away, and began bailing water. As she worked, the distressed girl kept scanning the bay, hoping she might see Nancy or George.

"They're both good swimmers. I'm sure they reached safety," she told herself hopefully.

But in a moment panic seized her again. What if the girls had not been swept from the cave. They might have been caught inside and drowned!

Her mind numbed by fear, Bess worked automatically on the boat, hardly taking her gaze from the water. She suddenly detected an object some distance away. Could it be a swimmer?

Leaping to a high rock, Bess shaded her eyes against the glare of the sun. Yes, someone was swimming feebly. Even as she looked, the person disappeared.

"Hold on! Don't give up!" she shouted, as the swimmer reappeared. "I'll reach you in a minute."

Rushing to the boat, Bess tried to start the motor. It was waterlogged and refused to catch. The oars had been washed overboard.

Kicking off her shoes, Bess plunged into the water.

"I'm coming!" she screamed. Then, "George!"

Bess reached her cousin not a moment too soon. George's strength was nearly gone.

"I'm—all—in," the girl gasped. "Hurt my arm."

Bess wasted no time in talk. She decided at once to use the swimmer's carry.

"Look into my eyes. Put your hands on my shoulders," she instructed quickly.

George obeyed, but at that instant a wave broke over the girls' heads. They were buried in an avalanche of water, and came up choking and fighting for breath.

"It's no use," gasped George, completely spent. "I can't make it. Save yourself."

Bess, realizing her cousin no longer could help herself, grasping her in the cross chest carry and pulled her through the water. But it seemed as if she could not possibly reach the shore. Burdened by George's weight, and with her own strength giving out, she found it harder and harder to keep going.

"But I *must* not fail," she told herself.

Then a wave, larger than any of the others, struck the two girls, lifted them up bodily, and wrenched them apart. It seemed impossible that they would ever reach shore.

But just as Bess was about to give up in despair, her feet came in contact with the beach. Standing up, she discovered that the water was only a little above her waist.

A short distance away George was being tumbled about in the breakers. Wading to her, Bess pulled the exhausted girl to safety. It was several moments before either one could speak. Finally George mumbled:

"Nancy— Is—she—safe?"

Fear for their missing friend drove Bess to her feet. Anxiously she looked about. Nancy was not in sight.

"Nancy—was—beside me—in the cave," she said brokenly. "That was the last I saw of her."

Tears rolled down the cheeks of the two girls. Each was silent with her own thoughts. Then suddenly Bess sprang towards the motorboat. She was just in time to prevent the rising tide from carrying it down White Cap Bay. As the girl tied the rope to a rock on the shore, she was startled to hear a faint "Hello" from the direction of the cliff above the cave.

"Nancy's voice!" she exclaimed joyfully. "She's safe! But where?"

Excitedly calling a reply, she and George waited eagerly for another shout. But it did not come. Bess waded into the water and looked up. Nancy was sitting high up on the cliff among the rocks.

"There she is!" Bess cried. "Thank goodness!"

George was so relieved, her strength returned at once. She got up, and together the girls shouted reassuringly to Nancy. But she did not seem to see or hear them. How were they to reach her?

"We'll have to use the boat," George decided. "Where are the oars?"

"Gone. And the motor won't start," Bess said forlornly. "But maybe I can dry it off."

In a watertight compartment under one of the seats she found a few dry rags which she used to wipe off the engine parts. After several sputters the motor finally started and they were able to get under way.

"Now where's Nancy?" Bess demanded, steering towards the mouth of the cave and looking up.

Their friend had disappeared!

Shouting her name several times, the cousins cruised back and forth near the base of the cliff. Nancy, however, did not reappear.

"She may have found a road up there and decided to hitchhike to the boathouse," George decided at length. "Let's go back."

Reaching the boathouse, the girls spied Nancy's roadster parked exactly where it had been left a few hours earlier. Their friend was not there, and the old fisherman from whom they had rented the motor-boat reported that she had not returned.

The man looked hard at the cousins. Although the hot sun had dried their clothing, they presented a very bedraggled appearance indeed. They replied to the old fisherman's questions briefly, but did not tell him of their mishap at Bald Head Cave. They thanked him for the use of the boat, paid him for it and the lost oars, and left.

"We must find Nancy," George declared anxiously. "Let's take the car and drive to the cliff. We may meet her on the road." Fortunately, she knew where Nancy kept an extra key to the automobile.

"But what about your arm?" Bess objected.

"It feels much better," George declared. "The numbness is gone now. I can move it."

Meanwhile, Nancy was making an effort to recover from her own frightening experience. The great rush of water had washed her out of the cave just behind George. Being a strong swimmer, she made her way back to the cliff and struggled for a handhold amid the rocks some distance from the entrance of the cave.

She pulled herself out of the water, and for a time lay panting on the rocks. Then, getting to her feet, she looked about in search of her friends. The uneven line of the cliff screened a good bit of the view, and she could see no one.

After shouting for her friends several times, Nancy

climbed higher. From this perch, she spied the motor-boat and Bess and George on the shore. Relieved that they were safe, she tried to figure out a way to reach them. It seemed best to climb to the top of the cliff and then scramble down the other side to her friends. When Nancy reached the top, she stood still to look around. Suddenly she began to feel light-headed and had to sit down.

"I'm getting to be a cissy," she scolded herself. "I must go on."

But Nancy seemed unable to move from the spot. She became so drowsy she had to lie down. The warm sun and a faint sweet aroma added to her drowsiness. Delightfully comfortable, she lost all count of time.

Then, as if from a long distance away, Nancy thought she heard voices. Two men seemed to be arguing violently. Or was she dreaming?

Pulling herself up to a sitting position with great effort, Nancy gazed about her. She could see no one. She must have imagined the voices.

"Am I going out of my mind?" she asked herself.

Then she promptly fell back on the rock and drifted off to unconsciousness.

· 6 · *Warning by Telephone*

DEEP in slumber, Nancy dreamed that she lay cushioned upon a soft, sweet-smelling meadow. Nearby sheep grazed peacefully, and the faint tinkle of bells came as music to her ears.

Presently two little brown elves crept from beneath a

bush and stared at her as if she were an intruder. Nancy heard one of them say:

"We can't allow her to stay here."

"We certainly can't," agreed the other elf whose voice was deeper. "We must move her before she wakes up."

Nancy tried to resist, but the elves seemed to have cast a spell over her. Powerless to move, she attempted to open her eyes but the lids felt as heavy as stones.

Borne upon the shoulders of the elves, she was carried a long distance. Then they put her down, but the couch was not a comfortable one. Something sharp cut into her back. Nancy rolled over, and suddenly was wide awake.

Sitting up, she gazed about her in utter bewilderment. Her clothing had dried in the sun but was very crumpled, reminding her of the struggle she had gone through to keep from drowning.

Nancy listened for the roar of the surf but could not hear it. The only sound was a low, humming noise which she finally traced to a nearby telephone pole. Then she discovered that she was in a roadside ditch strewn with sharp rocks and pebbles. Bayberry and other bushes shielded her view of a narrow dirt road.

"How did I get here?" thought Nancy, rubbing her eyes. "I remember climbing the cliff, but how did I cross the field to this ditch? The last I remember—let me see. Yes, I stretched out on a rock on the cliff."

Dimly she recalled the dream in which elves had transported her from her resting place. Had someone actually carried her to the roadside? She dismissed the possibility as fantastic.

Scrambling to her feet, Nancy gingerly tested her arms and legs. They were stiff and cramped, but she did not have a single scratch. Long exposure to the bright sun had tinted her face a deep pink, and her skin had begun to smart.

Retreating to the meagre shade of a dust-laden pine tree, Nancy debated a course of action. The countryside was unfamiliar, and she had no idea how far she might be from Candleton.

"Who knows, I may have been lying in that ditch for an hour or longer," she reasoned, not trusting the time on her water-soaked wrist watch. "I wonder what Bess and George thought when I didn't show up. Probably they went home. I must find a phone and talk to them!"

The nearest cottage was a quarter of a mile down the sun-baked road. Though confused by her experience, and frightened lest another lapse of memory overtake her, Nancy tramped pluckily through the thick dust.

At length she came to a weather-stained shingled cottage. Seeing an old-fashioned well in the yard, she crossed a cinder path to draw herself a cool drink and bathe her burning skin. A woman, whose face was as faded as the gingham apron she wore, peered curiously at her through the screen door.

"Land o' goshen!" the housewife exclaimed, coming outside. "You look all tuckered out! Have you walked far?"

Nancy replaced the tin cup from which she had been drinking and considered her reply carefully.

"Yes, I've walked a long distance," she said quietly. "My friends and I had an accident with our boat. May I use your telephone?"

"Bless you, we haven't one. The nearest phone is at the Gladstone Dairy, half a mile down the road." Nancy looked so discouraged that the housewife added kindly, "But do come in out of the hot sun. Sit down and tell me what happened. Are your friends safe?"

"I think so. We became separated. Where am I now? Far from Candleton?"

The woman stared at the girl curiously. "Don't you know?"

Nancy shook her head, dropping into a chair near the kitchen door. "I'm a stranger here. After the accident, I became confused."

"You're about three miles from Candleton, and a quarter mile from the bay. You weren't by any chance near Bald Head Cave when the accident occurred?" The woman's eyes opened wide.

Nancy realized that she had revealed too much. If she should tell the true story of what had happened, the tale would be enlarged by the superstitious people who had already feared the cave. And Nancy wanted no publicity.

"Is Bald Head Cave near here?" she countered innocently.

"Over yonder." The woman pointed in a south-easterly direction. "Fishing's good thereabouts," she added, "but you've got to be careful. Once my husband was in his boat near the cave entrance when a flood o' water came rushing out. He was lucky to get away alive."

Bald Head Cave was a subject Nancy did not care to discuss any further. Declining the offer of a glass of lemonade, she asked if there was anyone at the farm-house who could drive her to Candleton.

"I'll pay him well," she offered.

"Bless you, it's not a matter of money. My husband took a load of chickens to town and he isn't back yet. He'll likely drive in about sunset."

Nancy felt she could not wait. Even though a walk

to Candleton would mean gruelling punishment, she must attempt it.

Thanking the woman for her kindness, the determined girl started off. She felt much stronger now, and the sun did not seem so hot. Presently a car came speeding down the road towards her. It looked remarkably familiar.

"Why, that's my car!" she exclaimed.

Even as she shouted and waved, the driver braked and the car came to a halt. At the steering wheel was Ned Nickerson, a friend of Nancy's who was staying nearby and had stopped at Mrs Chantrey's to see her. Learning from Juno that the girls had gone to Bald Head Cave, he had driven to the boathouse intending to rent a boat and follow them. At the dock he had met Bess and George.

"Thank goodness, you're safe!" Ned cried, swinging open the car door and jumping to the ground.

Bess and George started to scramble into the back seat so that Nancy might sit beside Ned, but he vetoed this at once.

"Suppose you stay in front, and we'll climb in the back," he suggested. "I have a few questions I'd like to ask this young lady."

"Okay," said George, "but first I want to hear what happened to her."

Bess took the wheel and started for Candleton. Nancy, instead of telling of her adventure, asked eagerly.

"Has my father arrived?"

"Not yet," George shook her head.

"Any word from him?"

Again the answer was in the negative. Nancy's eyes filled with tears. She tried to brush them away before

Ned could see them, but she did not succeed.

"Please, Nancy," he said kindly, linking his arm through hers, "I'm sure your father is all right."

"But it isn't like him—"

"I know. Maybe he sent a message that never reached you."

"I hadn't thought of that," Nancy conceded. "You're probably right." She smiled up at the young man beside her. "I'm sorry you found me this way—"

"Well," he laughed, "you look all right to me. But suppose you tell us about your experience after you left the cave."

"You'll be amazed when you hear it."

Rather self-consciously Nancy related her strange dream and told of awakening in the roadside ditch. "I must have been completely out of my mind," she ended dismally. "I don't recall ever doing such a thing before in my life!"

"Perhaps you didn't wander in your sleep," Ned suggested. "You may have been carried."

"By elves? Oh, Ned!"

"By two man-sized elves. Notice anyone near the cave after the accident?"

"I wasn't in a state to observe anything." Nancy's blue eyes clouded with thought. "But I do recall—those voices—they sounded human!"

"Why do you suppose anyone would have carried you from the cliff?" George asked disbelievingly.

With a laugh, Nancy dismissed the subject, declaring, "All I know is that when I investigate Bald Head Cave again, I'll go prepared."

"And probably alone," Bess added darkly. "So far as I'm concerned, the mystery is welcome to remain forever unsolved."

Then seeing a roadside stand, she reminded the others that they had not eaten since breakfast. After a quick meal, which they all agreed could not compare with the Salsandee food, Bess drove on.

During the rest of the ride to Candleton, the three girls exchanged accounts of their strange and terrifying experiences inside the cave. All were sure that a warning bell had rung just before a flood of water rushed from within the cave.

"Why don't I try my luck there tomorrow?" Ned proposed.

"Don't even think about it!" Bess said, and was vigorously supported by George. "The cave is too dangerous!"

When they reached Candleton, Nancy, eager to learn if her father had written, asked that they stop at the post office. Quickly she fingered through the letters George brought from Mrs Chantrey's box.

"Nothing for any of us," she reported in disappointment. "Oh, now I'm sure something has happened to Dad!"

"Maybe there's a message at the house," Ned suggested kindly.

When they reached the Chantrey cottage, the young people heard the telephone ringing. As they walked up the porch steps, Juno, the maid, came to the door.

"Telephone for you, Miss Nancy," she announced. "A gentleman."

"There!" Bess exclaimed triumphantly. "It's your father, Nancy! All your worrying to no purpose."

Nancy raced into the hall.

"Hello, Dad?" she said eagerly into the transmitter.

But it was not her father who answered. The voice was that of a strange man.

"Listen carefully," he directed in clipped tones. "Your father requests that you meet him this afternoon at Fisher's Cove Hotel. Come as quickly as you can—alone."

"Who are you?" Nancy asked. "Why are you calling for my father?"

There was no answer. The stranger had hung up.

As Nancy turned slowly from the telephone, she found Ned standing behind her. Repeating the conversation, she asked for his advice.

"Don't go," he said instantly. "It's a trick."

"I'm afraid so myself, Ned. On the other hand, Dad may have a special reason for wanting me to meet him there. I must take a chance and go!"

"In that case I'll go with you."

"The man's instructions were that I come alone."

"Why alone, Nancy?"

"I had no chance to ask any questions. I only know I must obey instructions."

"If you insist upon going, I'll follow in my car," Ned decided.

While Nancy changed her clothing, he hastened to the village to have her automobile filled with petrol By the time he returned to the cottage, she was ready to leave.

Before Nancy could drive away, however, the telephone rang again. This time George answered it.

"Hello?" inquired an agitated femine voice at the other end of the line. "Has Nancy Drew started for Fisher's Cove yet?"

"Why, no, she's just leaving," George replied.

"Then stop her! Don't let her go!"

Before George could reply, the receiver clicked and the line went dead.

·7· Suspicious Actions

WITH mingled emotions, Nancy thought over the second telephone call. Common sense warned her she might be courting danger by driving to Fisher's Cove, but on the other hand, she was extremely anxious about her father.

"I'll carry out the first instructions, but I'll keep my wits about me," she decided. "If things look suspicious when I reach the hotel, I'll call the police."

Leaving Bess and George at the cottage to explain to their hostess what had happened, Nancy drove away. Ned kept close behind her in his own automobile, but as they approached Fisher's Cove he wisely put more distance between them.

Alone, Nancy drew up in front of a shabby, unpainted three-storey building which bore the name Fisher's Cove Hotel. A number of men, who were laughing loudly, sat on the front veranda. As she alighted from the car they eyed the attractive girl with an impolite scrutiny which embarrassed her.

"Dad never would have registered in a hotel such as this," she thought, hesitating.

Ned's car rounded the street corner. Reassured that she would not be alone, Nancy entered the building.

She walked up to the desk and asked the clerk for the number of Mr Drew's room. The clerk was about to reply when a flashily dressed man appeared. He rudely interrupted with a complaint that he had reserved a large room with bath and had been shown instead a small room with only running water. As she did not

43

wish to call attention to herself by protesting against the man's rudeness, she sat down and waited for the clerk to finish. Much better dressed than the hotel guests who filtered past, she felt herself a target for all eyes.

To Nancy's great relief Ned soon sauntered into the foyer and seated himself on the opposite side of the stuffy, smoke-filled room.

At that moment, an elderly woman with a mass of grey hair and wearing a flowered print dress, pushed close to her chair. As she passed, the stranger dropped a scrap of paper into Nancy's lap. Without speaking or giving any sign that she had noticed the girl, the woman walked on quickly, vanishing through a side exit.

Nancy read the paper at a glance. It said, "Your father is not here. Leave at once before you get into trouble."

"This is the second time I've been warned," she thought. "I'd be crazy to walk blindly into a trap. The only sensible thing to do now is call Mrs Chantrey and see if there's a message from Dad."

Since it seemed best not to do this in the hotel, Nancy went down the street to a drug store. The call took longer than she had anticipated, and was discouraging. No word had come. Upon returning to the foyer, she glanced towards the chair where Ned had been sitting. It was vacant and the young man was nowhere to be seen!

"Now where did he go?" the girl thought uneasily. "Perhaps I should have told him I was going to phone. Oh, dear, I don't like the idea of staying here alone!"

However, she started towards the desk. Before she could speak to the clerk, a well-dressed man in a grey suit approached her.

"Miss Drew?" he inquired.

"Why, yes."

"I am Doctor Warren." The man's manner was flawless, but the expression in his dark eyes disturbed Nancy. "Will you come with me, please?"

Instantly the girl was on her guard, suspicious of a trick.

"Why should I?" she inquired, studying the man carefully.

"Your father is very ill upstairs."

"Oh!" The news stunned Nancy, but she did not accept it completely. "Then why hasn't he been taken to a hospital?" she asked.

"Your father did not want to be moved at this time."

"Then you were the one who telephoned me?"

"No, but I asked the manager to call you. You do not trust me, my dear?"

The question caught Nancy unawares. She did not answer.

"Your silence tells me that you are distrustful," the man declared. "I cannot blame you. Suppose I have myself properly identified at the desk."

"Please," the girl said quickly.

Desperately she glanced about the lobby, wishing Ned would put in an appearance.

"Expecting someone?" inquired Doctor Warren.

"I'm just nervous," Nancy said, and her manner confirmed the words. "Is my father seriously ill? Tell me what happened."

"In a moment." The doctor took her by the arm, guiding her to the hotel desk. "First, I wish to reassure you as to my identity."

The clerk, an unpleasant-looking fellow with shiny, heavily oiled hair, was scanning the comic page of a New York newspaper.

"Hi, Doc!" he greeted the stranger, lowering his paper and staring almost insolently at Nancy.

"I wish you would tell this young lady who I am, Mr Slocum," the physician said.

"Sure. You're Doctor Warren."

"Are you satisfied now?" the man asked. Without giving Nancy an opportunity to question the clerk about her father, he steered her towards the stairway.

"Surely you're not afraid to come with me now?" he asked in an amused tone as she hung back.

"Why—no," Nancy stammered.

The identification should have satisfied her, but somehow it did not. Ned had not reappeared. If she accompanied Doctor Warren upstairs, only the hotel clerk would know where she had gone.

"Of course, if you don't wish to see your father—" began the physician.

"I do!" Nancy broke in. Suddenly she made up her mind that she was being entirely too cautious. "Take me to him at once!"

As she followed the doctor up the dusty, creaking stairs to a dingy second-floor hall, she looked about warily. Despite his reassurances, she wondered if she might not be walking straight into danger.

"It's all so weird," she thought. "Those two telephone calls! Then that strange woman who dropped the note into my lap! Who was she, and why did she tell me my father is not here? And what became of Ned?"

Ned at that very moment was frantically searching for Nancy. He had observed the strange actions of the grey-haired woman in the flowered silk dress. He had seen her drop the note into Nancy's lap, and had noted the girl's agitation.

"It's a trick of some sort!" he thought instantly.

Alarmed when Nancy left the hotel, he jumped to the conclusion she had either accompanied or followed the elderly woman. Hastening to the street, he looked round to see where they had gone.

Nancy was not in sight. Some distance away, however, he saw the elderly woman enter a building.

Ned decided to follow her. Hastening down the street, he was somewhat disconcerted to note that the building she had entered was a beauty salon. Heavy blue draperies curtained the front windows, making it impossible to see inside.

"I wonder if Nancy went in there too?" he thought uneasily.

Posting himself across the street, Ned waited and watched. Minutes elapsed. No one entered or left the beauty shop. Finally the young man could bear the suspense no longer.

Recrossing the street, he rather diffidently opened the door of the shop. Two girls who were passing by at the moment stared at him and giggled. Ned's face turned red.

"The heck!" he muttered angrily, but did not retreat.

Inside the only persons visible were an attendant and a customer who sat beneath one of the hair driers. By no stretch of the imagination did either of them resemble the woman who had entered the shop.

"I beg your pardon," Ned said to the attendant who came to the desk. "I'm looking for a grey-haired woman who entered here a few minutes ago."

"No grey-haired woman came into our shop."

"But I saw her," Ned insisted. "She wore a flowered dress."

"Are you sure she didn't stop next door at the bakery shop?"

"Well—I was a good distance up the street, but I thought she came in here."

"Sorry, you must be mistaken," the attendant said with finality.

Ned apologized for having intruded and looked in the bakery. No one was in there but a salesgirl, so he walked back swiftly to the hotel. As he had feared, Nancy was not in the foyer.

At his wits' end, Ned questioned two strange men and a newspaper vendor. The latter offered him a slim clue.

"I saw a pretty lookin' blonde goin' up the stairway with a man. She acted like she was upset."

"That might have been Nancy!" Ned thought.

The hotel had no elevator. Climbing the stairs to the first floor, the young man peered up and down the deserted hallway. No one was in sight, not even a cleaning maid.

"There's only one way to find out if Nancy's here," he thought. "I may as well start knocking on doors."

He tapped firmly on Room 224. When no one answered, he pounded harder. The door flew open and a sleepy-eyed, heavy-set man in dressing-gown and slippers glared at him.

"What d'you want?" he growled.

"I'm looking for a friend of mine—" Ned began, but the man cut him short.

"I don't know you or any of your friends. I'm tryin' to sleep, so clear out and leave a guy alone!" He slammed the door.

Ned tried the room to the right. Apparently it had not been rented, for although he rapped many times, no one answered.

Room 227 proved to be Ned's Waterloo. Before he could explain anything, an excited female whose hair rollers stood out like the spines of a porcupine, grasped him by the arm and gave him a shove down the hall.

"Listen, please let me explain," Ned pleaded.

"You'll explain to the police!"

To the young man's distress, the woman began to scream. Before he could calm her or retreat, doors began to open all along the hall. In the midst of the confusion, the hotel clerk appeared, flanked on either side by burly assistants.

"Okay, boys," he ordered. "Throw him out! He's causing a disturbance."

Ned resisted, but the two men seized him roughly by the shoulders and pulled him towards the stairway.

· 8 ·   *A Mysterious Malady*

MEANWHILE Nancy had followed Doctor Warren up the creaking stairway to the second floor of the hotel. As the man paused at a doorway midway down the dark hall, she could not hide her uneasiness.

"My dear, you really do distrust me," he said quietly.

"No," Nancy denied, ashamed of her misgivings. "It's only that so many strange things have occurred. For instance, that note—"

"Note?"

Nancy told him about the woman in the flowered dress who had slipped a message into her hand.

"I begin to understand your reluctance in believing me," said the doctor. Opening the door, he stood aside for Nancy to enter. "You are not walking into a trap," he added reassuringly.

Nancy smiled at him, and without hesitation crossed the threshold. Instantly her eyes focused upon a walnut bed which had been pulled up near the windows of the tiny, stuffy room.

"Hello, Nancy," a weak but familiar voice greeted her.

She ran to the bedside and grasped the hand of the pale, weak man who lay there. It was her father all right, but so changed that his appearance shocked her.

"So—glad—you—came, Nancy," Mr Drew murmured.

He smiled at her, pressed her hand, then closed his eyes as if in slumber. Badly frightened, Nancy turned questioning eyes upon the doctor.

"Your father's case is most puzzling," he said in an undertone. "After he was found practically unconscious by one of the hotel maids, the manager called me here to examine him."

"But how did my father get to this hotel, Doctor?" Nancy asked.

"By taxi, I was told. Apparently he was ill when he arrived. I've not asked many questions, for he insisted that he did not wish to talk about it until you came."

"Why didn't someone get in touch with me sooner?" the girl demanded.

The physician shrugged. "I wasn't called till this afternoon," he replied. "When your father asked to see you, I insisted upon the management calling you immediately."

"Has he been in this drowsy state ever since the maid found him?"

"Oh, no. At times he rallies strongly, then has a

relapse. Frankly, I can't explain it. I recommend that he be taken to a New York specialist for an expert diagnosis."

The name of the city seemed to rouse Mr Drew. His eyes fluttered open and he gazed quite steadily at Nancy as she knelt beside him.

"New York," he muttered. "That's where I was."

"Yes," Nancy jogged his memory, and waited for the rest of the story.

But Mr Drew, though he seemed stronger, was not inclined to talk in front of the doctor. "I must talk to you alone—alone," the lawyer said to his daughter.

Doctor Warren picked up his black bag from the dressing-table. "If you need me, I can be reached by phone at Garfield 438," he told Nancy. "Your father may remain strong and able to talk for several hours. If he has another sinking spell, call me at once."

"Of course," the girl nodded.

She asked how much they owed for his services and paid him. Then, grateful for his kindness, Nancy extended her hand.

"I'm sorry I was—so distrustful," she smiled.

"You were very wise," he said, "and you are a brave girl. Don't worry about your father. He seems much better now."

After the doctor had gone, Nancy returned to the bedside. To her alarm, her father tried to raise himself to a sitting position.

"No! No!" she chided, pushing him gently back on the pillows. "You must lie quiet."

"Nonsense!" he exclaimed impatiently. "I have something important to tell you. I must do it while I have the strength. I asked you to come here alone, because what I have to say is not for others to hear."

"What is it, Dad?" Nancy bent closer for his voice was almost inaudible. "You saw those men who cheated Mrs Chantrey?"

"Yes. Then I took the plane. We landed at a small airport about ten miles up the shore."

"What happened after that?"

"Started here by taxi, intending to phone you to drive over and get me. A woman who couldn't get a cab, rode with me."

"A woman?" Nancy inquired thoughtfully. "Can you describe her?"

"Stout—dark—not very talkative. Wore a big hat and veil. She left the cab at the outskirts of Fisher's Cove."

"Then where did you go?"

"Can't remember much after that. I became sleepy and must have dozed off. When I came to, I was in this bed. Some time later the doctor was called in. But this sickness is no mysterious malady, and I don't need any specialist to diagnose what is wrong with me."

"What do you mean, Dad?"

"I'm convinced I was drugged."

"Drugged! Not by the woman who rode with you in the taxi?"

"Probably by those two rascals I visited in New York. We had coffee together, and they may have given me a slow-acting sleeping powder. I recall when I told them I intended to prosecute to the limit unless they returned Mrs Chantrey's money, they left me alone for a while and went to another room to talk. When they returned they were very arrogant. I also remember—"

"Wait!" Nancy interrupted the story. "I think someone is at the door."

Crossing the room, she quickly jerked it open. No one was there, but she was positive someone had been eavesdropping.

Round the corner of the hallway, a woman crouched against the dingy plaster wall. A moment before, she had been listening at the keyhole of Mr Drew's room. Waiting until the door closed again, she noiselessly slipped away.

Descending the stairway to the first floor, the woman paused to see why a crowd had gathered in the hall. Ned Nickerson was protesting vigorously because hotel attendants were threatening to throw him out of the building.

"I'll not leave here until I find a certain girl and her father. If you put me out, I'll come back with the police!"

"Why didn't you say what you wanted?" the hotel clerk asked.

"You didn't give me a chance."

The woman who had descended from the second floor, pushed her way through the crowd to address Ned in a clipped, slightly nasal foreign accent.

"You search for bee-u-tiful blonde-head with eyes like ze stars?"

"Her eyes are blue, and she is—yes, she is pretty."

"Wearing ze dress of white?"

"Yes. You've seen her?"

"She left ze hotel long time past. She wait for monsieur in ze motor car perhaps?"

Thanking the dark-eyed stranger, the young man made his way downstairs to the street. But when he reached Nancy's roadster he did not find her waiting for him.

For a while Ned sat in the car, but as minutes elapsed

and still Nancy did not arrive, he became increasingly worried and restless.

"I was a fool to come down," he thought, suspicion springing up again. "I have a hunch that foreigner gave me a wrong tip."

At this very moment, Nancy, in the second floor room with her father, was trying to convince him that he should not get up and dress. In vain he argued that he felt strong enough to motor to Mrs Chantrey's home or at least to another hotel.

"I'm glad you've feeling better, but I doubt that the doctor would want you to get up so soon," Nancy said dubiously. "Why, you were practically unconscious when I arrived!"

"Just seeing you has helped me a lot, Nancy."

"I'll tell you what I'll do," his daughter offered, stalling for time. "Suppose I telephone Doctor Warren and ask his opinion? I also must settle your hotel bill."

"All right, but do hurry. I've had enough of this place."

"I'll be back as fast as I can. Don't stir from your bed until I return."

Nancy sped to the foyer. Doctor Warren's office did not answer her telephone call. As she left the booth, the hotel clerk motioned for her to come to the desk.

"You were asking about a Mr Drew a while ago?" he inquired.

"Yes. I found him on the second floor in Room 301."

"But we have no one here by that name," said the clerk, looking at the register. "Room 301 is assigned to Mr John Blake."

"May I see the register, please?"

Reluctantly the clerk pointed to an entry where a

John Blake had registered for Room 301. The handwriting was unfamiliar to Nancy.

"This isn't my father's signature!" she exclaimed. "Who brought him here?"

The clerk shrugged. "That I can't say," he said with a sneer. "I wasn't on duty. Maybe I'm all wrong."

Nancy was certain the man was lying. Nevertheless, she paid the bill, which was far in excess of what it should have been. Making no protest, she tried once more without success to reach Doctor Warren by telephone. Failing, she climbed the stairs to tap on Room 301.

"It's Nancy," she called, as Mr Drew did not answer.

Alarmed because there was no reply she pushed open the door.

"Oh!" she cried in dismay.

The bed was empty and had been remade. Mr Drew was not there!

Nancy rushed to the wardrobe, jerking open the door. Only a row of empty wire hangers greeted her gaze. Her father's clothing and overnight bag had disappeared.

·9· *A Frantic Search*

As NANCY gazed about the deserted room, she felt weak. Where was her sick father?

Badly frightened, and trying to decide what to do next, Nancy moved over to the window. Chancing to glance down into the courtyard, she was astonished to see a young man pacing slowly back and forth on the grassy plot.

Ned!

Her first impulse was to call out, but she thought better of this, and merely rapped on the windowpane. Hearing her, Ned glanced upwards. Nancy put her fingers to her lips and motioned for him to come up.

"Be right with you!" he silently formed the words, and noted the exact location of the room.

Nancy waited anxiously at the door for Ned. Several minutes elapsed. Then she heard footsteps in the hallway and angry voices.

"Now listen!" argued a man who the girl guessed was the hotel clerk. "Haven't you made enough disturbance around here?"

"Someone I'm looking for is in this hotel. I intend to find her!"

At that moment, Nancy opened the door and Ned rushed forward.

Nearly in tears, Nancy told him what had happened. The callous Mr Slocum listened coldly, and openly displayed annoyance as she suggested that Mr Drew might have wandered into an unoccupied room.

"Very unlikely," he tried to dismiss the matter. "In any case it's not our responsibility."

"You have a responsibility in helping me find my father, who is ill!" Nancy corrected him, her eyes flashing. "How many vacant rooms are on this floor?"

"I don't know without looking at the register."

"Are vacant rooms always kept locked?"

"They should be."

"But are they?" Nancy persisted.

"Not always."

"Then my father easily could have wandered into one of them. We must search for him."

"There's no sense in it," argued Slocum angrily.

"Perhaps you prefer to have the police do the investigating?" Ned cut in coldly.

The reference to police brought speedy results. Although the hotel clerk muttered beneath his breath, terming Ned a nuisance, he quickly produced his keys.

Beginning with the room directly across the hall, he tapped on doors and opened one after another. Dust stood thick on the furniture and beds had been stripped of linen.

"You see, it's a waste of time," Slocum grumbled. "Nobody here."

Nancy paid no heed. She had been examining faint footprints in the hall and now paused before a door at the end of the corridor. "Is this room occupied?" she asked.

The clerk could not remember. Without waiting, Nancy tried the door and found it unlocked. The room was dark, with curtains drawn at the windows. On the bed lay a man fully dressed, and sound asleep.

"He's probably been working all night, and is sleeping late. You'd better watch out!" Slocum said nastily.

But Nancy had recognized her father. With a cry of relief she darted to his side. Her first attempts to awaken Mr Drew brought no results.

Ned turned on a light. "Your father acts as if he's been drugged," he observed. Then he spied the overnight bag which stood by the door. "Wonder if all your father's things are in his bag?"

"I don't know," Nancy replied. "And there are several other things I don't know, too."

As she shook her father again, his eyes opened, and he yawned as if wakening from a pleasant slumber.

With an effort, the lawyer roused himself. "Why, hello, Nancy!" he greeted her. "Are we ready to leave?"

Then he turned over and went to sleep again.

Only after Nancy and Ned had tried for several minutes were they able to waken Mr Drew. He drank a glass of cold water, which seemed to revive him.

"Now tell me how you got in here," Nancy urged. "Did you dress yourself after I left?"

"Why, yes, I think so," he answered, trying hard to remember. "Then the girl came."

"What girl? You don't mean me?"

"No, the chambermaid. She wanted to make the bed and clean the room. I sat down to wait, and that's all I remember until you woke me up."

"You don't know whether you walked in here by yourself or were carried?"

"Now who would move him?" cut in the hotel clerk. "That's the craziest thing you've said yet."

"He was in 301," said Nancy.

"John Blake was in there. You said yourself you didn't recognize the signature in the register. Furthermore," Slocum added, turning to Mr Drew, "you're all mixed up about the chambermaid. The girls on this floor don't start work until just about now."

Mr Drew gazed at the man with sudden dislike. "That happens to be a point about which I am very clear," he said in a cold voice. "A dark-haired chambermaid entered my room to change the bed linen."

"You can identify her, I suppose?" the clerk asked insolently.

"I can if I see her again. How many girls work here as maids?"

"Four come on duty at this hour. Three others work the night shift, but they're not here yet."

"Send the girls to me, please. I should like to ask them a few questions."

Slocum looked annoyed for a moment, then a slightly sardonic grin played round the corners of his mouth.

"Okay," he muttered, "but you're making a lot of trouble round here."

A short time later four chambermaids, who could not understand why they were being summoned, came into the bedroom. Mr Drew asked each girl a few questions, then permitted her to leave. He had to admit he had never seen any of the maids before.

"Perhaps the woman who came to your room only posed as a chambermaid," Nancy suggested after the last girl had gone. "You may have enemies who followed you to this hotel."

Mr Drew nodded agreement. "Let's get away from here," he urged. "The sooner the better."

Nancy suggested that he should go to a hospital, but the lawyer assured her he was feeling much better.

"I want to go on to Candleton," he said stubbornly. "If I can walk to the car, a few days on the beach will make me as fit as a fiddle again."

To prove that he felt stronger, Mr Drew walked across the room twice. His steps were very uncertain. Nancy and Ned exchanged worried glances. At his insistence, however, they finally agreed to take him away. Nancy said she would telephone Doctor Warren and tell him of the change in their plans and bring the car to the rear entrance of the hotel.

"Your bill is paid so we can slip away quietly," she declared. "Ned, will you stay with Dad?"

"I shan't leave him a for second," he promised. "Signal with two toots of the horn when you're ready with the car."

Nancy told Doctor Warren of her father's improved condition and their decision to leave. She mentioned nothing of what had happened after his visit and hung up before he could make any objection to the arrangements.

Within five minutes Nancy had her roadster waiting at the hotel door. Not until her father was safely seated in the car did she relax.

"I'll follow close behind you in my car," Ned assured her. "I doubt that anyone will try to stop us now, but it's just as well to play safe."

Without further adventure, the two cars reached Candleton safely. Mr Drew, instead of showing signs of weariness or illness, actually seemed improved after the ride. And after he was settled in a downstairs bedroom of Mrs Chantrey's home, he insisted he felt as well as ever.

The next morning, before anyone was out of bed, Mr Drew dressed, slipped out of the house, and went for a long walk on the beach.

"Outwitted my keepers, didn't I?" he chuckled upon his return. "Now I've had enough of this invalid nonsense. Haven't you young folks anything to do?"

Satisfied that her father was his former self once more, Nancy joined her friends for a swim. The young people enjoyed an hour in White Cape Bay, then went back to the cottage to change their clothing.

Mr Drew was sipping a lemonade, deeply engrossed in a book. Nancy and Ned decided to go for a drive in the country for a few hours. Upon their return to Candleton, Ned parked the car on the main street and the two young people walked along looking at the shops. Ned paused before the window of a novelty jewellery shop.

"While I'm here, Nancy, I'd like to buy you a present. Something to remind you of your stay at Candleton."

Nancy blushingly shook her head. "I really don't need anything," she replied, smiling.

Just then the girl heard the familiar tinkle of a little bell. She turned her head quickly. Madame and her attractive cosmetic pushcart were coming up the street!

"Say, there's something!" Ned exclaimed, mistaking Nancy's intent scrutiny of the woman for an interest in her products. "Perfume and cosmetics! How about a pretty compact and some perfume?"

"I've seen these things before," replied Nancy, keeping her voice low. "Ned, they're very expensive and I believe not much good. I don't want anything that woman has for sale. Thank you, just the same."

Ned could not hide his disappointment. Glancing at the cart, he observed Madame with renewed interest. Her dark-skinned face was shaded by an elaborate flowered hat.

"Say, who is she?" he inquired. "I've seen her before somewhere, but I don't recall her pushing a fancy cart!"

"We might ask her where you met her," Nancy teased.

Madame, who was now opposite them, did not seem to recognize either the young man or the girl. She quickly pushed her cart past the couple and hurried down the street. Or was she only pretending not to know them?

"Maybe you're acquainted with her friend?" Ned questioned Nancy suddenly, his eyes twinkling.

A stocky man had emerged from the shadow of a nearby doorway, and joined the woman at the next corner. Both glanced back towards the young people.

"No, I never saw him before," Nancy replied, but she knew she would not forget his face. It was cruel and calculating.

The stranger made no attempt to buy any of the Frenchwoman's cosmetics or perfumes. Apparently they were well acquainted, for they conversed freely. They gestured angrily, and Ned and Nancy guessed he was trying to force the woman to agree to something against her will. Once Madame pointed towards the young couple. Wrathfully the man pulled down her arm.

"What do you make of it?" Ned asked curiously.

Nancy had no answer. Even as he spoke, Madame and her companion hurriedly walked away together, disappearing in the direction of the beach.

· 10 · *Story of a Bell*

NANCY and her father sat alone on the porch of the Chantrey cottage. Ned had left, Bess and George were at the movies, and their hostess had not returned from her day's work at the tearoom.

"It's wonderful to be here with you, Dad," the girl said affectionately. "But I'm getting a bit restless. You hinted at my being able to help you on Mrs Chantrey's case. You haven't given me my job yet."

"That's right, Nancy. But you must admit I was delayed in carrying on my own work. Thanks to you, though, I got out of that awful hotel. Now I can continue where I left off."

"Have you talked to Mrs Chantrey about the stock transaction, Dad?"

"Yes, and she took the news like a soldier. Harry Tyrox and his gang cheated her out of a lot of money and they must be prosecuted. I didn't tell her I'm afraid she'll never get any of her money back, but I believe she suspects it."

The lawyer went on to say that he regretted seeing Mrs Chantrey work so hard, and how deplorable it was that she had spent her savings so unwisely.

"The job I had for you concerns Mrs Chantrey herself, Nancy," Mr Drew went on. "I'm afraid if someone doesn't bolster her morale, she may break down."

"Oh!" escaped Nancy's lips. Then, "Sh, Dad, here she comes."

Mrs Chantrey walked up the porch steps, looking very tired. Nancy asked about her day at the Salsandee Shop, and she admitted she was having trouble again with her help. A waitress had given up her job without notice, and one of the shop's most reliable cooks had had an accident and was unable to work.

"I don't know what I'll do," the tearoom owner sighed.

"Since I didn't mix up too many orders last time, Mrs Chantrey, why not use me again?" Nancy volunteered. "I'd love to help, and I'm sure Bess and George would, too."

"It isn't fair to you girls," their hostess protested. "Didn't I invite you here for a vacation?"

"And we're having a grand one!" Nancy declared. "Why, it's fun at the Salsandee Shop. And I have another reason for wanting to work there," the girl added. "I'm especially interested in one of your customers."

"The odd old man who dropped the paper telling about the XXX bell with the jewels in it?" guessed Mrs Chantrey with a smile.

"That's right. Did he ever come to claim it?"

"No, he has never returned. The paper is still in the drawer at the shop."

Early the next morning, Bess, George and Nancy donned uniforms and once more took up their duties at the tearoom. The work was strenuous but they enjoyed it.

At noon Nancy watched for the odd old man who had sat at her table once before. But he did not come. Nancy wondered if she would ever meet him again. She was very much pleased, therefore, when late that afternoon she saw the man come in. He paused at the cashier's desk, and Nancy heard him say in an agitated voice:

"My name is Hendrick—Amos Hendrick, though I've been called A. H. all my life. Only this morning I discovered the loss of a certain paper. It's valuable, and I'll pay a good reward to get it back. I'm not certain I lost it here, but there's a chance it dropped from my pocket when I paid my bill."

"I'll ask about it, Mr Hendrick," the cashier replied.

"A. H., if you please," the eccentric man said firmly. "I don't like to be called Hendrick."

There was no need for the cashier to ask about the paper. Nancy identified the old man as the person who had sat at the table where she had found the strange paper.

"And you're the pretty little waitress who served me so nicely and asked so many questions about bells," the stranger chuckled.

As Nancy recalled she had merely listened attentively to his story and hadn't asked many questions, but she did not correct him. Instead, she said she would get the paper at once.

Nancy searched the desk drawer where the mysterious

message had been placed. She fingered through bills and invoices without coming upon it, then searched the other drawers. The paper could not be found. Neither Mrs Chantrey nor any of the employees was able to throw light on its disappearance.

Mr Hendrick plainly was distressed. "That paper is very old and valuable," he mumbled. "I wouldn't have lost it for a thousand dollars."

Equally troubled by the loss, Nancy did not know what to say.

"Don't you remember the contents of the message?" she inquired.

" 'Course I do. That paper was found in my father's safe when he died and I know the contents by heart. Thunderation! Do you think I want it to fall into the hands of a stranger?"

"Then you believe that some other person may be interested in searching for one of those XXX bells?"

A. H. gave her a quick, guarded look but did not answer. Edging towards the door, he muttered, "I do too much talking for my own good."

George, who had joined the group with Bess, intercepted the elderly man. "You're making a mistake if you don't tell Nancy Drew here all about your mysterious paper and get her to help you!" she exclaimed impulsively. "Why, she's solved more mysteries than you could count!"

The man paused. His eyes sparkled as he said, "Ganging up on me, eh? You girls are three peas in a pod, or I'm no judge. Now why are you so interested in that paper I lost?"

"Because we like mystery and adventure," Bess supplied eagerly. "Surely you've heard about Nancy Drew. After she solved the Crumbling Wall case, her picture was in half the papers in the country!"

"Bess!" remonstrated Nancy, embarrassed.

"Well, it's true!"

Mr Hendrick had not seen the articles, but his interest was roused. He asked many questions about the detective work Nancy had done. She was uncertain whether he was joking or serious when he inquired:

"Well, how much will you charge to take my case? It's a tough one, I warn you."

"I solve mysteries for the fun of it," Nancy laughed. "Suppose you tell me about your case, Mr Hendrick."

"Not here."

"We might go for a walk along the beach."

"Fine," agreed Mr Hendrick with enthusiasm. "Come along, all of you."

Walking a short distance down the shore, the girls led the old man to a seat on a half-rotted log amid the dunes.

"To make a long story short, I've been interested in bells all my life," he began. "So was my father and his father before him. Know anything about bells?"

"Only that they ring," giggled Bess.

"No two ring alike. Some are high-pitched, some low, some have beautiful tone quality, and others are so harsh they insult your ears. Bells are with us from the cradle to the grave; they rejoice in our victories and toll our sorrows. They have enriched historical moments, coloured romance, and struck terror in the hearts of the superstitious. They even tinkle from the ankles of dancing girls!"

Bess and George stole a glance at Nancy, for they thought the man who insisted upon being called A. H. was a trifle touched on the subject of bells. Their friend, however, was deeply impressed.

"My father was a bellmaker and so was my grand-father," A. H. resumed proudly. "They learned the art in Europe, where they had their foundry. Know how to make a big bell?"

Nancy replied that she had only a vague idea.

"First you make a mould, and that takes a good many weeks if the bell is to be a perfect one. Then you pour in the hot, liquid metal. You have to be very careful. If the mould is not properly constructed, or you don't wait until the metal sets properly, the bell will crack when you take it out. A large bell must be cooled for a week or two before it can be removed."

"Tell us about American bells," Nancy urged, wishing to draw Mr Hendrick into revealing more about the mystery.

"The first bell foundry in this country was established by the Hanks family, ancestors of Abraham Lincoln on his mother's side," Mr Hendrick related. "Then there was Paul Revere. After the Revolution, he built a furnace in Boston and cast small bells. He also made large ones for churches. During his lifetime he cast nigh up to two hundred bells."

"What became of them?" inquired Nancy innocently.

"Ah! There lies the story. Fifty were destroyed by fire, one hangs in King's Chapel, Boston, but most of the others are lost. By that I mean, they're scattered over the country, and the folks that own 'em probably don't realize what a treasure they possess."

"Do you collect bells?" Bess inquired.

"Yes, I do. I've toured the country up and down looking for them. Own maybe fifty bells of all types and construction, but the one I'm after eludes me."

"The XXX bell with embedded jewels?" Nancy supplied softly.

A. H. nodded. "That paper I lost was found in my father's effects and was written in my grandfather's hand. The bell was stolen from my grandfather's foundry. I've spent more than eight years searching for that bell."

"You've found no clues?" asked George.

"I found some, but nothing came of them. My search has been interesting, though. I've collected other valuable bells, and I've met a lot of nice folks. I use the Paul Revere story to get them to talk. Usually they end up by showing me all the worthless bells on the premises."

"There's one bell I wonder if you have seen," said Nancy thoughtfully. "According to the stories round here, it hangs somewhere deep within Bald Head Cave."

"Oh, I heard that story when I first came here," the old man answered carelessly. "Nothing to it."

"Why do you say that?"

"Because I went there and looked round."

"And you didn't hear the bell?"

"No bell rang and no ghost appeared to warn me," A. H. chuckled. "It's just one of those superstitious tales. Want to hear a yarn about the bells of Notre Dame?"

Nancy was far more interested in keeping the conversation centred upon Bald Head Cave, but she listened politely to the story the old man told. When he concluded, she said quietly:

"About Bald Head Cave. I can't understand why you didn't hear the bell. When my friends and I went there, we not only heard the warning bell, but we barely escaped with our lives."

Instantly Mr Hendrick became attentive, asking many questions.

"I must go there again!" he exclaimed. "Tomorrow, perhaps."

"You'd better take us with you," Nancy suggested. "After our experience I'm sure you shouldn't go there alone."

A. H. chuckled. "I can't swim a stroke, I admit. Maybe I could use the help of three athletic girls if I should get in a tight spot with that ghost!"

Arrangements were made to meet the old man the following afternoon at one of the boat rental docks. The girls arrived ten minutes ahead of time. Amos Hendrick soon ambled along.

"I want it thoroughly understood before we start," Bess announced as she climbed into the boat, "that we're not setting foot inside the cave. It's too dangerous! We can hear the bell without going inside!"

"Agreed," said A. H. "But I warn you, if I should hear a bell ringing, no telling what I'll do."

Nancy took the helm of the motorboat and they made a speedy trip to the foot of Bald Head Cliff. No fishermen were nearby, and the entire shore appeared to be deserted. Nancy shut off the motor, allowing the boat to drift close to the shore.

"Don't go any nearer the cave," Bess warned, becoming nervous. "It's dangerous."

A. H. said nothing, but from the way he smiled the girls knew he considered them overcautious. For half an hour Nancy kept the boat hovering near the cave entrance. Nothing happened.

"I'm getting tired," Mr Hendrick complained. "Why don't we go ashore and—"

He broke off, listening intently. Nancy and her frinds also had heard the sound. Deep within the cave a bell tolled mournfully.

"It *is* a bell!" cried the old man excitedly. "A mighty good bell, too, with fine resonance and tone quality! It sounds like those my grandfather made years ago!"

Forgetting the girls' warning, he seized an oar and started paddling the motorboat into the cave.

"No! No!" exclaimed Nancy, grabbing his arm. "We mustn't disregard the warning!"

"I must get that bell!"

A. H. climbed to the gunwale to jump out!

· 11 ·   *The Deserted Cottage*

WITH a mighty jerk Nancy pulled the eccentric old man back into the boat. A moment later a great flood of water rushed from the cave. The boat was buffeted wildly by the waves.

"The ghost must have seen us!" exclaimed Bess dramatically, gripping the side of the boat to keep from being tossed into the water.

Amos Hendrick, who a moment earlier had scoffed at the ghost tale, now was trembling like a leaf. As Nancy steered the craft into less turbulent water, he said with an attempt at composure:

"This brings to mind a story told me as a child. According to the tale, a worker in a bell foundry near the ocean set sail in a small boat equipped with a tolling bell. It was said he joined some pirates who hid their loot in a cave. Nothing was ever heard about him again."

"Perhaps he was drowned at sea," Nancy suggested.

"So it was assumed. Because for many years, on moonlight nights, other workers reported seeing his ghost walking on the water not far from the foundry."

"And you believe the story?" George asked.

"I do. Many persons vouched for the tale. The ghost finally disappeared, and it was said he went back to the cave."

Bess and George winked at Nancy. They were convinced A. H. was obsessed with the subject of bells. As if to confirm their suspicion, he quoted absently:

"A wizard of such dreadful fame
That when in Salamanca's cave,
Him listed his magic wand to wave,
The bells would ring in Notre Dame!"

"That's from 'Lay of the Last Minstrel,'" A. H. explained, and then added with a quick change back to the present, "I'd like to get my hands on that bell inside Bald Head Cave!"

"Please don't try," Nancy requested. "It's too dangerous."

"Let's go home," proposed Bess. "This place makes me feel uneasy."

"I have something I want to do first," said Nancy, staring speculatively at the cliff. "Who wants to go exploring?"

"I for one," replied George promptly.

Bess, less eager, said she would accompany her friends. But Mr Hendrick declined the invitation to go with them.

"I haven't enough of the goat in me to climb up and around rocks. You girls go along by yourselves. I'll stay here and watch the boat."

"Don't let the ghost get you," George said jokingly, as they stripped off shoes and socks before wading ashore.

Leaving the man behind, the three companions reached the rocky beach. There they put on their shoes again. Bess started up the cliff ahead of the others, unwisely choosing a steep trail. Suddenly she slipped, and with a scream began to slide down the incline.

Hearing the cry, Nancy looked up. Her heart jumped. Bess was headed for the sharp rocks below! She would be killed if something did not break her fall.

Nancy braced herself firmly and looked about for something to hold on to. Seeing an outcropping bush, she seized it firmly in one hand. As Bess slid against her, she put her free arm about the girl. The two teetered precariously on the edge of the cliff for a few seconds, then regained their balance.

"Wow! That was a close call!" Bess said trembling. "Thanks, Nancy."

George, who had been watching from below, hurried up the path to scold her cousin.

"Bess, you must be more careful!" she warned her. "Both of you might have been dashed to pieces!"

"I know it," Bess agreed. "No more rock climbing for me! I'll sit right here and wait until you girls get back."

Nancy and George left her and climbed swiftly but with caution. Reaching the top of the cliff they admired the view, and waved to A. H., who sat in the drifting boat.

"I came up here a much easier way the day we nearly drowned in the cave," Nancy said. "Want to see where I had that remarkable dream?"

"So that's why we made the climb!" scoffed George. "I'm curious to find out how the place looks, now that I have my wits about me."

Without difficulty Nancy spotted the general location where she had slept.

"I can't figure out how you reached the road from here," George commented. "If you walked in your sleep you were lucky you didn't fall off the cliff and kill yourself."

"I think so too," Nancy said soberly.

The two girls wandered about, seeking a trail which would lead to the road. Before they had gone many yards, George stumbled into a crevice between the rocks, severely twisting her ankle. Though she tried to walk, it was evident she could go no farther without great pain.

"I'll hobble back towards Bess," she decided. "You go on by yourself, Nancy."

Nancy hesitated, but George, who knew her friend wished to do some more exploring, would not permit her to give up the expedition.

Nancy went on alone, directing her steps towards a weather-beaten cottage nestled against high rocks. She did not recall seeing it the first time she was on the cliff, probably because of the drowsy state she was in that day.

"What a strange place for anyone to live!" she reflected. "No trees. No garden. It must be cold and windy in the winter."

Impulsively Nancy decided to call on the occupants. It was not until she was quite near the cottage that it suddenly occurred to her the men whose voices she had heard might live there.

Nancy was tempted to go back, but as she gazed at the house she began to feel sure that it was deserted. The curtains at the windows looked very soiled. A painted rocker stood on the porch, dust-covered and faded. It swayed gently to and fro in the wind as if occupied by someone invisible.

Nancy went to the door and knocked several times. No one answered. Convinced that the house was vacant, she tried the door. Finding it had no lock, she lifted the latch and went inside.

What Nancy saw caused her to draw in her breath sharply. Chills raced down her spine.

A dining table which stood in the centre of the room was set with two places. Food lay on the plates. But the food was mouldy and covered with cobwebs. A chair stood precisely at each place, as though the occupants had gone away suddenly just before sitting down to the meal.

"Some tragedy must have occurred here," Nancy reasoned. "And not recently, either. The owners must have left the cottage in a hurry, never to return. But why?"

Peering into the other rooms, the girl saw further evidence that the former tenants had fled quickly.

"It's strange they never came back to remove the furniture," she mused.

Deeply impressed, Nancy left quietly, carefully closing the outside door so that it would not bang back and forth in the wind. Reflecting upon the strange appearance of the house inside, she made her way slowly across the cliff. Midway to the spot where she had left George, she was startled to hear a scream.

"That was Bess!" Nancy thought, recognizing her friend's voice. "Now what has happened?"

She started to run. From afar she could see George, who looked greatly excited.

"Perhaps Bess fell again!" Nancy told herself.

Out of breath and thoroughly frightened, she reached the spot where George was standing.

"What is it?" she cried. "What's wrong?"

George answered by pointing towards the bay.

The motorboat, with only the eccentric old man

A. H. aboard, was chugging off rapidly in the direction of Candleton!

· 12 ·   *Stranded*

"WHAT's the matter with A. H.?" George cried furiously. "He can't go off and leave us stranded here!"

"Maybe he can't, but that's exactly what he's doing!"

Sharing George's alarm, Nancy cupped her hands and called to the eccentric old man. If he heard her, he gave no sign.

From some distance below, Bess also was shouting and waving. It seemed incredible that A. H. could not hear her.

"He's going off and leaving us on purpose!" George cried bitterly.

To be left alone on the cliff was a serious matter. There were no boats, and the nearest inhabited house was a long distance down the road. George, with an injured ankle, could not walk even a quarter of the way.

They watched, hopeful that the motorboat would turn and come back for them. Instead, it kept on steadily towards Candleton. Soon it was a mere speck on the water.

"There's only one thing to do," Nancy said. "You and Bess stay here and wait. I'll go for help."

"Where?"

"If necessary, to that house where I stopped the other day. Perhaps there's a cottage closer."

"Maybe I could walk." George gazed dubiously at her ankle, which had become badly swollen.

"You never could make it, George."

Telling Bess of the plan, Nancy overruled her offer to go along. "No, you stay with George," she urged.

The sun was still high overhead and beat down upon the rocks. As Nancy set off to bring help to her friends, she could not stifle a feeling of resentment towards Amos Hendrick. What had possessed the peculiar old man to leave them stranded?

"He must have had some reason," she thought. "I don't believe he would abandon us on purpose. When I see him again—Oh!"

Nancy stopped short. Unconsciously she had turned in the direction of the abandoned cottage. From afar she could see the door flapping in the wind.

"That's funny!" she thought. "I know I latched that door."

A dark shadow fitted round the side of the cottage. Nancy's eyes opened wide. Had someone left the house, or was the figure that of some animal?

"It must have been my imagination," she decided. "But just to make certain, I'll walk over there and find out."

The weather-stained cottage was as deserted looking as when she had seen it before. Again she knocked. Again no one appeared. Once more she pulled the door shut and tested the latch to be sure it would not open again.

Before leaving, Nancy hurriedly circled the house, but saw no one. Yet she was uneasy.

"The wind couldn't have opened the door," she reflected. "It isn't strong enough. And that shadow—"

In a hurry to reach Candleton, Nancy did not wait any longer. Striking out in what she judged to be the right direction, she was relieved to come upon a path which led out to a dirt highway. A quarter of a mile farther on Nancy reached the spot where she had awakened on her previous trip.

"How in the world could I have wandered such a distance in my sleep?" she asked herself. "It seems impossible."

Before long Nancy came to the same farmhouse she had visited before. This time a car stood in the yard, its engine running. A man, evidently the owner of the place, was about to start off.

"Wait!" Nancy hailed him.

He pulled up at the gate.

"Are you going to Candleton?" the girl asked breathlessly.

"That's right."

"May I ride with you?"

"Sure. Hop in." Dusting off the seat, the farmer swung open the door.

As the car bounced over the rough road, Nancy told him what had happened, explaining that she meant to hire another boat and return to the cliff for her stranded companions.

"By the way, who lives in the cottage on the cliff?" she inquired, hoping to pick up a little useful information.

"Why, nobody."

"I mean, who were the former occupants before the cottage was abandoned?" Nancy corrected herself.

"Sorry, but I can't tell you. My wife and I only came here a few months ago. We don't get around much or see any of our neighbours. Too busy trying to make a living from our farm."

They soon reached Candleton, and at Nancy's request the farmer obligingly dropped her off at the waterfront. He would accept no pay for the drive, insisting that it had not inconvenienced him in the least.

Hastening to the wharf where she had rented the motorboat, Nancy saw that the craft in which A. H. had abandoned them had been returned. But where was he? Seeking the owner of the boat, she asked him if he had seen Mr Hendrick.

"Sure, he came in about an hour ago," the man replied.

"Did he leave any message or give any reason for going off in the boat and deserting my friends and me at Bald Head Cliff?"

"Why, no! You mean to tell me he deliberately left you girls in that forsaken spot?"

"He certainly did. I came to town for help. My friends are still there on the rocks, one with an injured ankle."

"That was a mean trick. I can't understand it. Take the boat and go after your friends. Do you need any help?"

"No, I can manage alone. Thanks just the same."

The boat owner filled the tank for Nancy, and to make certain she would be prepared for any emergency, tossed in an extra can of fuel, a bailer and a life preserver.

Although visibility was good on the water, late afternoon shadows were beginning to darken the shore line. At full speed she proceeded to Bald Head Cave, anxiously scanning the cliff for a glimpse of her chums.

To her relief she saw a flash of colour amid the rocks at the base. George and Bess were waiting for her on the beach.

Overjoyed to see her, they shouted and waved. Supported by Bess, George limped through the shallow water to climb aboard the boat.

"We thought you'd never get here," Bess sighed. "Did you see A. H. while you were in Candleton?"

Nancy shook her head.

"Just wait until I see him again!" George said angrily. "I'll tell him a thing or two!"

"I still think he must have had a reason for deserting us the way he did," Nancy said. "How did you get along after I left?"

"Okay," replied George. "It was hot on the rocks, but my ankle feels better now."

"No ghostly apparitions?"

"Not one."

"How about the bell inside the cave?"

"We listened for it," Bess said, "but didn't hear a sound. Apparently the ghost only goes into action when you're on the scene, Nancy!"

Without further delay the girls sped directly to the boat dock and took a taxi to Mrs Chantrey's cottage. Mr Drew, obviously upset, was restlessly walking about outside when they arrived.

"Why, Dad!" Nancy exclaimed, alarmed lest he might have had a recurrence of the strange ailment from which he had suffered while in Fisher's Cove. "Is anything wrong?"

"I'm disgusted! Thoroughly disgusted! Read this!"

The lawyer thrust a telegram into his daughter's hand. It had been sent from New York and was from one of the young assistants in his office. As Nancy read the message, her heart skipped a beat.

AS PER YOUR INSTRUCTIONS CALLED ON BROKERS AT OFFICE AND HOTEL. THEY HAVE SKIPPED. AWAIT FURTHER ORDERS.

"That's dreadful, Dad."

"Indeed it is! It ruins all my plans. I hardly know which way to turn," Mr Drew said.

"At least it proves they're dishonest. That will help strengthen your case against them, won't it?" Nancy asked, trying to soften the blow for him.

"Yes, dear, that's true. The mistake I made was in giving Tyrox and the others a chance to make good. They should have been told nothing until I was ready to prosecute. Now they've taken Mrs Chantrey's money and probably that of other investors as well and vanished!"

"You've never told me much about the case, Dad. What kind of stock was it Mrs Chantrey bought?"

"The stock has no listing on any exchange. In my opinion, the entire transaction was a swindle. I do wish Mrs Chantrey had asked my advice before she bought shares in a worthless perfume company."

"A perfume company?"

"Yes, a salesman showed her an impressive report of the firm's earnings which I'm sure was a fake. She thought she was buying into an old, well-established company dealing in exclusive French products of high quality.

"What's the name of the firm, Dad?"

"The *Mon Coeur* Perfume Company."

Nancy stared at her father, scarcely believing he had spoken a name so familiar to her. Mr Drew noted his daughter's startled expression.

"Don't tell me you know anything about that company!" he exclaimed.

"I've seen the *Mon Coeur* products," Nancy replied. "There's a woman right here in Candleton who sells them. And I've seen a man, whose looks I don't like, on the street with her!"

It was Mr Drew's turn to stare.

"He may be Harry Tyrox, one of the swindlers I'm after! He's the head of the company. Nancy, do you think you can find him for me?"

· 13 ·   *The Chemist's Report*

WHILE Nancy was telling her father everything she knew about Madame and her pushcart of cosmetics, Ned drove up and joined the Drews. He listened in amazement to the story.

"Did that woman speak with a French accent?" he asked suddenly.

"Yes."

"And was she dark-skinned, wore her black hair slicked back, and had a mole on her left cheek?"

"That's a very accurate description," Nancy agreed. "But I didn't know you were close enough to her to make such a minute observation when we saw her the other day."

"I wasn't!"

"Then don't keep us guessing. Where did you see her before?"

"At the hotel in Fisher's Cove. When we saw that woman with the pushcart I thought her face looked familiar. Ever since I've tried to remember where I had seen her before."

"She may have recognized you, Ned. That would explain why she hurried away so fast. Where was she in the hotel?"

"On the first floor when I was arguing with the

clerk. This woman came down from the second floor and told me you had left the hotel."

"From the second floor?" Nancy repeated thoughtfully.

"Yes. I should have been suspicious, but it didn't occur to me until later that it was a trick to get me away from the hotel."

"It certainly looks as if you've hit upon a good clue to locate the *Mon Coeur* crowd," Mr Drew reflected. "Let's take the car and see if we can find that woman with the pushcart."

For an hour the three searched high and low throughout Candleton, asking for Madame. No one had seen her for several days.

"She probably left town after she saw us, Ned," Nancy ventured. "Maybe she went back to Fisher's Cove."

"And you'd like to go there to find out," Ned smiled. "How about you folks having dinner with me there?"

Mr Drew declined, saying he expected a telephone call from his young assistant who was in New York. He knew Nancy and Ned were fully capable of handling any situation should they locate Madame.

The three returned to the Chantrey cottage. While Nancy bathed and changed her clothes, Ned talked with Bess and George, and politely asked them to accompany him and Nancy. They thanked him but refused, saying they had promised to help Mrs Chantrey, and left to have dinner at the Salsandee Shop.

"Shall we eat along the way or wait until we get to Fisher's Cove?" Ned questioned as he and Nancy drove off.

"To be truthful, I'm dreadfully hungry," Nancy confessed. "I haven't eaten for hours. There's an attractive place about five miles from here."

"I know the one you mean," Ned answered. "They have a good music group. We'll stop there."

It was nearly nine o'clock when they finished eating. Ned was reluctant to leave the good music and dancing, but finally they went on to Fisher's Cove and parked near the old hotel.

"Don't get into another fuss with the clerk," Nancy teased him as they went inside.

"If that fellow gets smart with you or me, I may have to."

The interview with Mr Slocum, who was on duty, started badly. When Ned asked if a woman answering the description of Madame had registered there, the man was as uncommunicative as before.

"I don't know who you're talking about," he retorted, "and furthermore, I don't care. All I ask is that you two quit bothering me."

"It should be of importance to you to know the kind of people who frequent your hotel," Ned said with dignity.

"I'll have no slurs on this hotel!" the clerk shot back. "The people who come here are all right—"

Ned bristled, but Nancy restrained him, saying:

"We're not accomplishing a thing this way. Let's go."

"Slocum knows more than he'll tell," said Ned as they walked away from the desk.

"Perhaps. But let's not make a scene."

Ned grudgingly acknowledged that Nancy was right. She told him that she had another plan for getting the information, and they left the hotel. Seeking a telephone, she called her father, telling him of Slocum's attitude.

"How about putting a plain-clothes man in the hotel to watch everyone who enters or leaves the place? Madame or Harry Tyrox may come in."

"Not a bad idea," agreed Mr Drew. "In fact, since we don't know the woman's name, it seems about the only way to spot her. I'll arrange it."

Nancy was not too hopeful that the plan would bring results. As she remarked to Ned on the way back to Candleton, it seemed reasonable that if the *Mon Coeur* crooks ever had made their headquarters at Fisher's Cove Hotel, they certainly had moved out by this time.

"Isn't it possible Madame is peddling her products in other small towns around?" Ned speculated.

"Very possible. I mean to do some investigating in them."

"And I'll make a date with you right now to help, Nancy."

The girl laughed. "But I want to start out right after breakfast tomorrow."

"That's okay with me."

"But can you get up that early?"

"I certainly can!"

"There's no putting you off I see," Nancy chuckled. "All right. Nine-thirty in the morning."

Ned was there promptly and they set off. The couple visited one seashore resort after another, but the trip netted nothing in their search for the promoters of *Mon Coeur* products. No one had seen Madame in days, although she had covered the countryside selling cosmetics.

"At least we're following her trail," Nancy said, refusing to be discouraged.

They were standing in front of a drug store window which prominently displayed *Mon Coeur* powder and perfume. "Perhaps we ought to warn this chemist not to buy any more of the products."

"These may be better than the stuff Madame sells from her cart," Ned suggested. "It's possible she gets good perfume and dilutes it to make a high profit for herself."

"I hadn't thought of that. Suppose I buy some of these and have them analyzed?"

"Good idea," approved Ned. "I have a college friend not far from Candleton who will make the report for us, and we can depend on it being accurate."

Nancy purchased a lipstick, a box of powder, and a small vial of perfume. Later that afternoon Ned took them to his friend, Bert Hamilton, who lived a few miles down the shore. Only two years out of Emerson College, which Ned now attended, the young man already had made a name for himself as a chemist.

"Bert promises us a report by tomorrow night," Ned told Nancy upon his return. "I took the liberty of suggesting he bring it over to Candleton. He's going to get hold of Bill Malcome—you remember him. We'll make it a sixsome and go over to the Yacht Club dance. Okay?"

"Sounds like fun," Nancy smiled. "I'm sure Bess and George would love it, too."

When the cousins heard about the date, they were very pleased. Both knew Bill. In fact he had escorted George to several parties in River Heights.

The following evening the girls were just finishing dressing when the boys arrived. Nancy ran downstairs ahead of the others to greet their guests, who already were talking with Mr Drew. Ned presented Bert, who seemed to be a likable person.

"Did you bring the report?" Nancy asked him at the first break in the conversation.

"I can give it to you in a few words," the chemist replied. "The sample of perfume was mostly water."

"I thought so!" exclaimed Nancy.

"The face powder contained chalk—the common schoolroom variety—mixed with a little ordinary rice powder to give it texture. The lipstick contains a cheap substance, which really is a poison to the skin. It's dangerous to use."

Nancy had asked Ned not to mention their suspicions regarding the *Mon Coeur* manufacturers. She herself merely said:

"Wait until poor Bess hears this! She spent a lot of money on those products."

Bess came downstairs at this moment and met the chemist. The tru.n of his findings was not easy for her to accept. She was ashamed to think she had not followed Nancy's and George's advice.

"I'd like to know what the perfume is like," Mr Drew spoke up. "Would you mind getting your bottle, Bess?"

The girl hastened to her room, and returned with the vial she had purchased from Madame. As she uncorked it, a strange, not too pleasant fragrance permeated the air.

"The dreadful stuff gets worse the longer it stands!" George declared.

"Why, how funny—" the lawyer started to say, then stopped. He put the back of one hand across his eyes.

"Mr Drew, you're not feeling ill again!" Bess exclaimed.

The lawyer sank into a chair, staring into space. Alarmed, Nancy darted to his side.

"Dad!"

"I'm quite all right, my dear," her father said. "But that perfume—"

"Cork the bottle," George ordered her cousin.

"No, no, that's not necessary," said the lawyer. "The perfume doesn't bother me. But I connect it with something unpleasant."

"In what way, Dad?" Nancy asked.

Mr Drew seemed lost in thought for several seconds. Then suddenly he snapped his fingers.

"I have it! I remember now!" he cried excitedly. "The woman in the taxi with me! She used that same perfume!"

· 14 ·   *The Candlemaker's Help*

As THE other young people went outside to get into the cars, Nancy and Ned hung behind to talk further with Mr Drew about the woman in the taxi.

"You're sure she had on *Mon Coeur* perfume?" the girl asked her father.

"Positive."

Nancy asked him to describe the woman again. The lawyer said he had not paid much attention to her, but recalled she was dark, had rather large features, and wore a veil.

"She could have been Madame," his daughter said excitedly. "Dad, you thought those *Mon Coeur* men in New York might have given you a slow-acting drug. Perhaps Madame was their accomplice at this end of the line."

"You're probably right," Mr Drew agreed.

"It's even possible—" said Nancy, then stopped.

"What were you going to say?" prompted her father.

"It seems fantastic—but then so do a lot of things that have happened lately—but maybe you weren't drugged in New York at all. Perhaps the woman in the taxi did it."

"But how? I didn't swallow anything."

"With the perfume."

"You mean the woman disguised something like— well, like ether, with that sweet-smelling perfume?"

"Yes."

At this moment an automobile horn began to toot loudly, and shouts of "Nancy! Ned!" reached their ears.

"You'd better go along," the lawyer urged. "I'll talk to you in the morning. Good night, Ned."

For several hours Nancy enjoyed the music and dancing at the Candleton Yacht Club. When they reached home, she, Bess, and George tumbled into bed to awaken rather late the next morning. As Nancy came downstairs, she heard her father telephoning the airport.

"You're going away?" she asked, when he hung up.

"I must leave at once for New York, but I'll return as soon as I can," he promised. "My assistant picked up what may be an important clue."

"About the *Mon Coeur* people?"

"Yes, Nancy. I haven't time to explain the details. A neighbour is taking me to the airport. Will you pack a few things in my bag?"

"Then I'm to stay here?"

"Yes, I've already talked with Mrs Chantrey. She won't hear of you or your friends leaving. You're to remain and work on the mystery. You don't mind?" he added, a twinkle in his eye.

"Maybe I'll have the whole thing solved by the time

you return. And the mystery of the tolling bell, too,"
Nancy countered, hugging her father affectionately.

She ran upstairs to pack his bag, and a few minutes
afterwards he rode away. Bess and George appeared a
little later and were surprised to hear of Mr Drew's
departure.

"Hurry up and eat. We ought to get started," Nancy
said suddenly.

"Started where?" Bess wanted to know.

"I want to go and talk to Mother Mathilda, the
candlemaker Mrs Chantrey told us about. She's supposed to know everything that's happened round here
for the past sixty years."

"And you think she can solve the mysteries?" George
scoffed, finishing a glass of orange juice Juno had
brought in.

"Maybe," Nancy grinned. "But seriously, Ned and I
scratched only the surface in our search for Madame.
If she's staying in some out-of-the-way place, Mother
Mathilda may know where."

"Also, you'd like to find out from her who lived in
that cottage on Bald Head Cliff, and why the people
went away in such a hurry," Bess smiled.

"And learn a little more about the ghost in the cave,"
added George with a wink at her cousin.

The three girls set off on foot for the old section of
Candleton. They exclaimed over the quaint houses and
shops, declaring that walking down Whippoorwill Way
was like stepping into another era.

Finally, passing a moss-covered stone church, the
girls came to an old-fashioned dwelling of pounded
oyster-shell laid brick. Attached to it at the rear was a
fairly new wooden lean-to, which marred the otherwise
picturesque lines of the house.

"This is the place," announced Nancy, noting a wrought-iron sign which said "Mathilda Greeley. Hand-poured, perfumed candles for sale."

They rang the doorbell. When no one came, the girls circled the building to investigate the lean-to at the rear.

"Why, it's the shed where the candles are made!" exclaimed Nancy, peering through the open doorway.

From the ceiling hung hundreds of gaily coloured wax candles of all lengths and sizes. Near the door were bright scarlet ones, and beyond blue, yellow, pink and green.

"Doesn't it remind you of a rainbow?" gasped Bess in delight.

At the rear of the room, a bent-over old lady with white hair and crinkly skin stood with her back to the girls. She was stirring a kettle of hot, green-coloured wax.

"Oh, dear! What shall I do?" the woman mumbled to herself.

Nancy tapped lightly on the door before crossing the threshold. At the sound of footsteps, Mother Mathilda turned and nodded for them to walk in.

"We're staying with Mrs Chantrey," explained Nancy, smiling. "She suggested we come here."

"Oh, yes, I have heard of you." The old lady went on stirring. "Look around. You don't have to buy."

Nancy and her chums became aware of a familiar but faint odour. Nancy asked what it was.

"I have been making perfumed candles," Mother Mathilda replied, "but they are a failure. The entire lot is ruined! Not in thirty years have I had such a loss."

"Are they bayberry candles?" Bess asked, since the colour of the liquid was green.

"Oh, no, my bayberry candles are the only ones which turned out well this week."

The old lady pointed to a rack of delightfully fragrant tapers, explaining they had been made by cooking berries, skimming off the wax, refining it, and pouring it onto strings suspended from nails.

"Isn't that a rather unusual way of making candles?" Nancy asked. "I thought they were always made in moulds, or else the wick was dipped into hot wax."

"You're right," agreed the old lady. "But years ago my family perfected the method of pouring the liquid onto the wick. When one layer hardens, we put on another coat. But I was the one who added the perfume," she announced proudly. "And never in the thirty years that I've been making sweet-scented candles have I had a failure until now."

Mother Mathilda explained that after she had added a newly purchased perfume to her "batter," it not only did not hold well to the wick, but the candles did not have the fragrance they should.

Nancy noticed three large empty bottles on a shelf above the kettle. They bore the *Mon Coeur* trademark.

"Did you use the perfume from these bottles?" she inquired.

"Yes. I bought them from a woman who claimed her products were superior to any other on the market. But I am burdening you with my troubles! You came to buy candles, or to see how they are made."

"We do want to buy some of the bayberry variety," Nancy replied. "What really brought us here though is to ask you about that very woman who sold you the perfume."

Mother Mathilda looked surprised. Then she said, "There is little to tell. The woman, a foreigner, came here and gave me samples of a lovely oil. It seemed exactly what I needed for my candles, so later I bought a large supply. But the perfume was inferior to the oil."

"What a shame!" murmured Bess. "That woman is a fraud and a cheat. She has sold worthless perfume all along the coast."

"Have you any idea where she is?" Nancy asked Mother Mathilda.

"No. I asked several of my neighbours, but no one knows."

"It won't be easy to trace her, I'm afraid," Nancy said, worried. "Once she cheats a person, she's wise enough not to return."

She and her friends could find little to say to comfort Mother Mathilda. They were afraid she never would recover a penny of the money she had given to Madame for the worthless perfume.

"It must have been only Madame's perfume that was of poor quality," the old lady went on in a more hopeful voice. "Ordinarily, *Mon Coeur* products are of the best."

Nancy stared at her curiously. "Why do you say that? Have you used them before?"

"No, but Monsieur who sold me stock in the company showed me testimonials signed by a dozen film stars praising their products."

The words stunned Nancy and her friends.

"You also bought *Mon Coeur* stock?" the Drew girl asked, hoping she had misunderstood.

"Twenty shares. Monsieur Pappier, president of the company, sold them to me himself. Oh, he was a fine, elegant gentleman! He kissed my hand and made very pretty speeches." Mother Mathilda blushed as she said this.

"Can you describe him?" Nancy asked.

"Monsieur was a stout man with plump, apple-red cheeks. He wore a velvet jacket with braid. His voice sounded husky as if he had a sore throat."

"My father may know the man. The description fits a certain Harry Tyrox, wanted in New York for a similar sale of *Mon Coeur* stock."

"You don't think the man is an impostor?"

"I am afraid he is, Mother Mathilda. Did anyone else in this neighbourhood buy stock?"

"Oh my, yes! Maude Pullet, my next door neighbour. And Sara Belle Flossenger, the seamstress, took forty shares. Then the tailor, Sam Metts, bought some."

"What a day for Monsieur Pappier!" commented Nancy grimly. "I'm sorry to tell you that the stock he sold has no value."

"Oh, it can't be true! There must be some mistake! Almost all my life savings were given to that man!" gasped the woman, sinking into a chair.

As Mother Mathilda wept softly, Nancy told her who she was, and attempted to comfort the woman by saying Mr Drew was trying to trace the stock swindlers.

"Nancy is working on the case, too," added George. "I'm sure those awful men will be caught."

After some time the girls succeeded in cheering up the old lady a little. They bought several dozen bayberry candles, and changed the subject of conversation.

"Who used to live in the cottage on the top of Bald Head Cliff?" Nancy asked the candlemaker.

"Oh, you mean the old Maguire place!"

"Is that the name of the people who lived there? Did they leave suddenly for some reason?" Nancy pursued the subject.

The question seemed to surprise Mother Mathilda. "Why, not unless you'd call going to their heavenly reward suddenlike," she commented. "Grandpa Maguire and his wife died from old age. But so far as I know, the son and his wife are still there."

"The place is deserted."

"Then the report that they moved away must be true. I couldn't believe it," remarked the old lady.

"You knew the Maguires well?"

"As well as I knew my own mother. Grandpa was quite a character!" The old lady chuckled. "He had a flowing white beard that reached to his knees. And how he did like to spin yarns! He was a lookout in the old days."

"Lookout?" Nancy questioned.

"Grandpa Maguire had a powerful telescope," Mother Mathilda explained, "and he'd sit on his porch, watching the sea for returning fishermen in their boats. Whenever he'd spy one, he'd scramble across those rocks nimble as a goat, and drive to town to tell the women. Then they'd come down to the sea to meet their menfolks."

"What became of the telescope?" Nancy asked, recalling the man who had gazed at them through one the first time she and her friends had gone to the cave.

"I don't know," the candlemaker replied. "Do you want me to find out for you?"

"Thank you, no," Nancy answered. "I was just wondering."

Actually she was wondering whether the man on the cliff might have been using the Maguire telescope, and if so, where it was. She had not noticed it lying anywhere in the cottage during her hurried inspection of the place.

Nancy discussed her idea with Bess and George as they walked home. George thought the man with the telescope might have been Mr Hendrick.

"He's a strange old fellow," she declared. "I'll bet he knows the secret of that cottage."

"I agree," said Bess. "When he saw us climb the cliff and head towards the deserted cottage he went away in the boat. Perhaps he thought that would distract us from our investigations. He might have been afraid that we'd discover something he didn't want us to know."

"But he may have enemies, too," added George. "Who else would have stolen the paper he dropped in the tearoom?"

Nancy had to admit there was something to her friends' theory. She was determined to find A. H. and learn what she could from him. Even if he said he had never been on the cliff, at least he owed them an explanation for running off with the boat.

But Amos Hendrick seemed to have vanished from Candleton. The girls inquired at the boat rental dock, stores, and boarding houses. No one had seen the man. Finally the three friends went to the Salsandee Shop and ate an early luncheon. Mrs Chantrey, learning they were there, asked if they would go on an errand for her.

"I've just had a phone call from Maplecrest Farm," she said. "They were to bring me a crate of berries, but their truck has broken down. Will you drive over and get the berries for me?"

Nancy said they would be very glad to and got her car. She headed for Maplecrest Farm which was situated about two miles out of town on the shore opposite the cliffs. As she sped along, Nancy passed a parked car. No one was in it, but down by the water, a hundred yards away, two men stood talking.

Their backs were turned to the girls, and it was not until Nancy drove into the farm lane a few minutes later that she suddenly thought she recognized the men.

"A. H. and the fellow I saw talking to Madame!" she cried aloud.

"Honestly?" exclaimed George.

"I'm going to find out!" Nancy declared.

"How about the berries?" Bess asked. "Mrs Chant—"

"I'll get them. Take the money out of my bag for me, will you, Bess?"

Nancy accomplished the errand in less than two minutes, much to the amazement of the owner of the farm. She quickly turned the car round and raced out of the lane to the highway.

· 15 · Minnie's Awakening

As NANCY sped back to the spot where she had seen the two men talking, she kept hoping they were still there.

"I wish I'd stopped before," she said to Bess and George. "Probably they've gone by this time."

They were gone. There was not a sign of the men nor the car. Bess tried to console Nancy by saying she doubted the men could have been A. H. or Madame's friend. George, meanwhile, had spied a boat chugging slowly away from the shore.

"Look, Nancy, maybe the fellow in there is one of the men you saw!" she suggested. "He's going towards Candleton. Let's find out!"

Nancy put on more power and they skimmed along the road. Reaching the Salsandee Shop, the girls left the crate of berries at the kitchen door and hurried off again.

"Now where are we going?" Bess asked. "That man at the dock told us A. H. hadn't rented a boat, so he won't come in there."

Nancy felt that the old bell collector probably had hired a boat from one of the fishermen.

"I suggest we go over to the wharves where the fishermen are and find out," she said.

Upon their arrival, Nancy made inquiries and learned that her guess was right. Mr Hendrick had rented a dory only an hour before.

"What a surprise he's going to get when he sees us," George laughed. "Three detectives ready to pounce on him!"

When A. H. reached the wharf, the girls expected him to try to avoid them, but the eccentric man greeted them with a smile and said:

"Well, I'm glad to see you. That saves me a trip. I was going to call on you and offer my apologies."

"We did expect to hear from you and learn why you took our boat and left us stranded on the cliff," Nancy told him.

Amos Hendrick hung his head. "I'm right sorry about that," he said. "The truth is, I suddenly remembered I had an appointment. I couldn't wait for you girls any longer."

"Was it with the same man you saw today?" Nancy shot at him.

The bell collector looked surprised and asked how she knew that. Nancy explained vaguely.

"Yes, it was the same man," A. H. answered. "The other time Mr James didn't show up."

"Mr James who?" George interposed.

M.T.B.

"James is his last name." A. H. leaned forward and whispered confidentially, "He has a bell I might buy."

"Oh!" said Nancy. Then she asked, "What does the man look like?"

"Oh, kind of red-faced. Has a stocky build and dark hair. Why?"

Nancy evaded the question. "I might want to talk to him myself sometime about bells," she answered non-committally.

Inwardly she was very excited. The description definitely fitted the person with whom Madame had been talking! Mr Hendrick started to move off, but Nancy was not through questioning him. She wanted to know about another matter also. She asked him when he had last driven to the cliff above Bald Head Cave.

"Cliff?" the man repeated. "I've never been up on those rocks and don't intend to go. Nothing there worth going for that I know of."

"We thought we saw you up there looking through a telescope," said Bess.

"Not me. And where would I get a telescope? Well, I must go now," he smiled. "Hope you've forgiven me for running off with the boat."

After he had left Nancy felt that the interview had not been entirely satisfactory. Either Amos Hendrick was hiding some facts for reasons of his own, or else he was the victim of some hoax. She was sure the man who called himself Mr James and said he had a bell to sell was the one she had seen talking with

that man was Harry Tyrox," George He's connected with the *Mon Coeur*

Nancy shrugged. "I may have been mistaken," she said.

"What's next on the programme?" Bess asked. "Pleasure or mystery?"

"Couldn't the two go together?" Nancy laughed. "But seriously, what's next isn't going to be fun. I'm afraid it will be heartbreaking."

"Gracious, what is it?"

"I want to call on the people who bought stock in the perfume company from Monsieur Pappier."

Nancy had written down the names of the victims mentioned by Mother Mathilda. Because of her father's connection with the case, she felt she ought to see them and learn what she could. At least one of them might be able to give a clue to the whereabouts of the swindler who had taken their money.

"Do you want us to go with you?" Bess asked.

Nancy nodded. After learning from Mrs Chantrey where the people lived, the girls set out.

As Nancy had predicted, the calls were anything but pleasant. Maude Pullet wept on hearing the news. The little seamstress declared she felt too discouraged to try to save even a penny of money again. Sam Metts, white-faced and grim, told the girls that the swindle would cost his son a college education. At each home Nancy acquired the names and addresses of additional persons who had been cheated by Monsieur Pappier.

"This swindle is rolling like a snowball," she said excitedly to her friends. "Unless we check it, there's no telling how many others will lose their savings!"

Nancy kept hoping she might uncover a clue to the present address of either Monsieur Pappier or Madame. Such information was not forthcoming. The only one given by the people she interviewed was the New York office, vacated several days earlier.

Learning that several persons in the little country town of Branford had bought stock, Nancy motored there in the late afternoon with Bess and George. Interviews with two purchasers brought only the familiar story of fabulous profits which had been glibly promised by Monsieur Pappier and a companion salesman.

Discouraged, Nancy was leading the way to the parked car when she noticed a girl standing on the opposite side of the street.

"Isn't that the girl who bought some cosmetics from Madame?" she asked. "The one whose mother tried to have me arrested?"

"Yes," agreed George. "And look at the get up! Where did she find such outlandish clothes?"

The girl's face was made up heavily with lipstick and rouge. She wore a scarlet, sleeveless dress. It was unfashionably cut. High-heeled slippers with rhinestone buckles fitted her badly. As the girl walked down the street, she kept pausing every few steps to readjust the buckles.

The three crossed the street.

"Hello," Nancy greeted the girl with a friendly smile. "Aren't you a long way from home?"

"Not half far enough!" the girl retorted, tossing her head. "But I'll never go back, not even if Ma takes a horsewhip to me!"

"You've run away from home?" Nancy guessed.

"So what? I couldn't stand it on the farm another day. I've changed my name from Minnie to Hortense, and I have a fine job already!"

"In an office?" inquired Bess, wondering who would employ such a gaudily dressed person.

"No, as a model."

The three girls were speechless.

"I demonstrate *Mon Coeur* cosmetics for thirty dollars a week," Minnie went on proudly. "Madame is going to give me a bonus, too."

This information excited Nancy, but she was careful to keep her voice even as she asked, "Where do you give the demonstrations?"

"We'll have one tonight at nine o'clock in front of the Branford Hotel."

"Oh, not until tonight?"

"We never have our demonstrations until late," Minnie explained innocently. "Madame says the night light makes everyone look better." The girl giggled. "You ought to see me. I pretend to look awful, and then she fixes me up grand."

"I see," said Nancy, hiding a smile. "Well, I wish you good luck with your new work." Then she added carelessly. "I can see you like working for Madame."

"She's a fine woman!" Minnie retorted. "She gave me enough money to buy these clothes, and she lets me have all the perfume and cosmetics I want without charging me a cent!" Minnie teetered away on her spike heels.

"It's too bad we can't notify that girl's mother where she is!" exclaimed George, when the model was beyond hearing.

"I'll try to persuade her to go home," Nancy replied, "but not until after the demonstration tonight. Girls, do you realize Minnie may solve the mystery for us!"

"Will you notify the police to be on hand?" asked Bess.

"I may. How I wish Dad were here!"

"You have a date with Ned tonight," Bess said. "Why not talk it over with him?"

Nancy said she would. When Ned arrived and heard the news, he assured Nancy he was all the police force she needed.

"I can handle Madame," he laughed. "And Minnie, too. There's bound to be a constable not far away, if we want him to make any arrests."

Nancy was not completely satisfied. But she admitted to herself that the presence of the police might forewarn Madame or her accomplices.

She and Ned started off, and shortly before nine o'clock they reached the Branford Hotel and waited near the entrance. Soon Minnie appeared looking very unattractive in a black dress, her face pale, her lips colourless.

"She's certainly carrying out her part of the bargain," Nancy smiled.

"By the way, where is the pushcart woman?" inquired Ned, glancing towards a clock in the square. "It's ten minutes past nine now."

The seller of *Mon Coeur* cosmetics had not appeared. Even Minnie showed signs of increasing restlessness. She glanced uneasily up and down the street.

"I have a feeling Madame isn't going to show up!" commented Nancy presently, beginning to be fearful her plans would fall through.

"I have the same idea," said Ned.

At nine thirty-five Minnie suddenly lost patience. With an angry exclamation she started away from the hotel, convinced that her employer would not appear. This was the cue for Nancy and Ned to saunter forward and intercept her.

"Isn't there to be a demonstration?" Nancy inquired innocently.

"I can't give it alone!" the girl snapped. "And I haven't anything to sell. Oh, why doesn't Madame show up?"

"Maybe you'll never see her again," suggested Ned.

"I will so! Something must have kept her. I'll go to her home."

"You know where Madame lives?" Nancy could barely keep her voice calm.

In reply, Minnie took a paper from her purse and read the address aloud.

"We'll drive you there," said Nancy firmly.

·16·   *A Thwarted Scheme*

DURING the ride to the house where they hoped to find Madame, Minnie Glaser kept up a chatter which exhausted both Nancy and Ned. But as the car drove up in front of an old, dark house, Minnie suddenly became silent. Not a light shone from any of the windows.

"It looks as if it's deserted," Ned observed. "You two wait in the car while I find out."

He was gone over ten minutes. Nancy had started to wonder what had happened, when he returned and shook his head.

"No one there?" she inquired.

"No one except a caretaker. The owners have gone away for the summer."

"Madame has gone away!" exclaimed Minnie. "I know better than that!"

"I didn't say Madame was the owner of the house," Ned corrected the girl impatiently. "No such person has ever been here. The woman gave you a false address."

At first Minnie Glaser refused to believe the truth. When it finally dawned upon her that she had been tricked, the girl burst into tears. She had no place to go, she declared. Her last dollar had been spent on clothes.

"You could go home," Nancy suggested. "We'll take you there."

"And have my family laugh at me? Or whip me?"

"Isn't it better than having no place to sleep or eat?"

Because she had no choice, Minnie finally consented to being driven to her parents' farm. But as they neared the place, Nancy became more and more fearful of the reception they would receive.

"Suppose you go in alone," Nancy urged Minnie.

"Oh, no!" she exclaimed, clinging to Nancy.

As the car stopped, the door of the farmhouse flew open and Minnie's parents rushed out to see who was in it. When they saw their daughter they cried out in happiness, and as she stepped from the car Mrs Glaser took her child in her arms.

"Oh, Minnie, don't ever go away again!" she sobbed. "I know I've been harsh, but from now on you kin have more freedom."

Tears flowed freely down Minnie's cheeks. Then suddenly she remembered Ned and Nancy!

"These—these people made me come home," she said. "You can thank them."

Mr Glaser put out a gnarled hand, and his wife wiped her tears and said:

"Please excuse me. I've been so upset these past few days I forgot my manners. Thank you kindly for bringing Minnie back." She did not recognize Nancy, and the girl was rather glad of this.

Nancy and Ned left the Glaser family happy in their reunion. As they rode back towards Candleton, Nancy became very quiet.

"What's the matter, Nancy? Worried about something?" he asked.

"Just disappointed. I had such high hopes for solving part of the mystery tonight, but—"

"But instead, you helped a poor girl who needed help badly, and I admire you for it, Nancy."

"Thank you, Ned," Nancy smiled. Then she added, "You know what I mean, this mystery is so important."

After she reached home, Nancy continued to think about the strange puzzle. She wondered how her father was making out; where Madame had gone; how they could find Harry Tyrox; and when the mystery of the tolling bell would be solved.

The next morning Nancy was her usual cheerful self. But Bess and George knew she had something special on her mind, for she fairly raced round doing all sorts of unnecessary chores. With her friends she went to the Salsandee Shop early, and speedily helped Mrs Chantrey arrange garden flowers on the tables and prepare fruit before any of the regular employees arrived.

Soon patrons began coming in to breakfast. The first man to seat himself at Nancy's table was a dwarf-like fellow she had seen in the tearoom before. He gave his order in a gruff voice, then became absorbed in the morning paper.

As Nancy went back and forth from the kitchen, she kept stealing glances at the man. Where had she seen him before? To satisfy herself, she asked Mrs Chantrey about him.

"I don't know his name," the tearoom owner replied. "He's one of our most unfriendly customers. Never so much as says hello, although he comes here regularly. Evidently his wife is an invalid, for he always takes food for her when he leaves."

That night after the shop closed, Mrs Chantrey invited Nancy, Bess and George to a concert. The cousins accepted, but Nancy begged off, saying she would rather stay at the house as her father might telephone or even return. Juno was out and it was very quiet at the cottage. Nancy picked up a book, but instead of reading she sat lost in thought.

"Who *was* that man at the tearoom?" she asked herself over and over again.

Presently a car pulled up at the kerb outside the house. Thinking her father might have arrived by taxi, Nancy ran to the porch. But she was wrong. A stocky man with a dark moustache alighted, pulling his felt hat low over his eyes. Seeing the girl, he asked gruffly:

"Are you Nancy Drew?"

"I am."

"Then you're to come with me."

"For what reason, please?" The man's manner had made Nancy suspicious.

"Your father needs you. He's in trouble."

"I don't believe it and I won't go!"

"Oh, you won't, eh?" the fellow growled, losing his temper. "Well, listen to me! You and that snooping father of yours had better mind your own business, or it'll be the worse for you both! Understand?"

The stranger advanced towards Nancy. Frightened, she ran into the house, slamming and locking the door. Turning off the lights, she stood behind the living-room draperies and watched the man from the window.

He started towards the door, but changed his mind. Returning to the parked car, he drove away, keeping close to the kerb as he disappeared down the street.

Nancy picked up a flashlight and ran outside to look around. Tyre tracks were plainly visible in the sandy road. As she examined the pattern left by the rubber tyres, her roving light revealed a small bundle lying close by.

"Here's something!" she thought, picking it up. "This must have fallen from the car when that man opened the door!"

Inside the cottage Nancy examined the package under a bright kitchen light. A crude sketch of three chiming bells in a cluster had been pencilled on the plain brown wrapping paper.

Puzzled, Nancy unwrapped the bundle. Hundreds of labels bearing the *Mon Coeur* trademark fluttered to the table and floor.

"So that man was one of the *Mon Coeur* crowd!" Nancy thought excitedly. She stared at the sketch on the paper. "I wonder if they're going to change their design from hearts to bells?"

The idea so intrigued Nancy she decided to try getting in touch with her father by telephone. At that moment the doorbell rang. Startled, Nancy tip-toed to the hall and peered through the window. Careful not to open the door, she called to the man on the porch. Then, she snapped on a desk light in the living-room and hastily penned a note to her friends. Leaving the message in plain view, the girl let herself out of the back door.

But in her haste to get away from the cottage, Nancy neglected to close a side window in the living-room. Scarcely had she gone, when a strong gust of wind caught her note and carried it beneath the couch.

Some time later, Mrs Chantrey, George and Bess came home to find Nancy absent and not a word to explain what had become of her. As the minutes became hours and she did not appear, they grew uneasy.

"Shouldn't we notify the police?" Bess asked anxiously. "Something must have happened to Nancy!"

George was inclined to agree to the proposal, when Mrs Chantrey called from the kitchen. She had just spied the package of *Mon Coeur* labels.

"How did these get here?" she asked in amazement.

Bess and George had no answer.

"Nancy must have had a visitor while while we were away!" Bess exclaimed fearfully. "Maybe she's been kidnapped!"

•17• *A New Trademark*

MRS CHANTREY could think of no reason for Nancy's long absence, but she was inclined to believe the girl was too resourceful to allow herself to be kidnapped.

"Why not wait a while longer before calling the police?" Mrs Chantrey suggested, and finally the girls consented.

When another hour passed, they were confronted with a new worry. A glance at the falling barometer warned of an approaching storm. The wind began to moan through the trees surrounding the house.

"I'm going to call the police," Mrs Chantrey said with sudden decision.

As she started towards the telephone, the storm broke

in full force. A mighty gust of wind swept through an open window, blowing a sheet of paper from beneath the couch.

"What's this?" exclaimed Bess, picking it up. "It's a note from Nancy!"

The others ran to her side. The brief message said: "Have gone out with Ned on important business."

"Maybe they've eloped," giggled Bess, glad the strain was over.

Not feeling entirely relieved, Mrs Chantrey closed the open windows and wiped the spattered woodwork. Rain fell in torrents. The water was running like a river in the streets.

"Wherever Nancy is, I hope she's not out in this storm," Mrs Chantrey said, pacing the floor.

George was inclined to believe that Nancy had gone with Ned to investigate a clue in connection with the *Mon Coeur* case. In this supposition she was right.

Earlier in the evening when Nancy heard the doorbell ring, she called through the window and discovered it was Ned. Briefly she told him of the strange man's visit and the package he had dropped.

"We must trail that man if we can!" she added. "But someone may be watching the house, so I'll slip out the back way and meet you over on the next street."

Ned was waiting in his car when she reached the appointed place.

"This may be a wild, useless chase," Nancy said breathlessly. "But I saw the man's car turn down this street when it left Mrs Chantrey's."

"Notice the make?"

"No, it was too dark to see the car plainly."

"Then how can we trace it?"

Playing the beam of her flashlight along the roadway

close to the kerb, Nancy did not answer.

"What are you looking for?" asked Ned, puzzled, as he got out of the car.

Nancy pointed to tyre tracks plainly visible in the sandy road. She explained that they were of the same pattern as those she had found in front of the Chantrey house after the man's car had pulled away.

"I noticed that the driver hugged the kerb," she added, "so we may be able to trace him."

"It's worth trying," Ned agreed, springing into the car again.

The tyre tracks led to a small print shop in an alley. There the car had turned in, apparently parked near the side entrance, and then had gone on.

Inside the building a light burned brightly. A man in a printer's apron could be seen working over one of the presses.

The thud of a hand press deadened the sound of their footsteps as Nancy and Ned entered the cluttered little shop. Not until they shouted did the stooped old man with grease smeared over his apron whirl round to face them.

"We may want some stationery printed," Nancy said as an excuse for the interruption. "Would it be possible for you to do it soon?"

"Miss, I couldn't even touch it for six weeks! Why, I'm wallowin' up to my ears now in commercial orders. That's why I'm puttin' in extra time tonight—trying to get caught up."

"Do you do much label printing?" Nancy asked casually.

"Makes up about fifty per cent of my business. Been doing a lot of work for the *Mon Coeur* people lately."

Nancy was careful not to show her elation at the

information. "Oh, yes, I understand they're putting out another line, too. What's their new trade-mark? Is it three bells or—"

She purposely hesitated, and the old man completed the sentence for her.

"You mean *Sweet Chimes*."

"Are you going to do the work for the firm?"

"No. I'm too rushed. Anyhow, that fast-talkin' foreigner, Monsieur Pappier, said he'd rather give the job to another printer who is closer to where the products are goin' to be made. Said it wouldn't pay him to have any more work done here."

"Where is the place?" Nancy asked, trying to keep down the excitement in her voice.

"Let me see. Was it New York—no, that wasn't it. Yorktown! Or maybe it was Yorkville. All I remember is, that it had a York in the name."

"Did Monsieur Pappier call on you tonight?"

"Yes, just before you came. This morning he picked up a package. He started talkin' about that *Sweet Chimes* idea, and he drew a sketch of the design on the wrapping paper. Tonight he came back saying he couldn't find his package. He thought maybe he'd forgotten to take it, but I guess he lost it."

"I think I've seen Monsieur Pappier," Nancy said. "Does he wear a moustache?"

"No," replied the old man. "Must be somebody else you have in mind."

"Probably," said Nancy. "I'm sorry we kept you so long from your work. Goodnight."

Nancy was excited as she and Ned returned to the car.

"It must have been Monsieur Pappier who called on me!" she remarked. "He put on a moustache for a disguise! And he didn't have a trace of a foreign accent. I'm convinced he's Harry Tyrox!"

"Maybe he changes his nationality at will," suggested Ned.

Although it was now after eleven o'clock, Nancy had no intention of abandoning the chase. Consulting a road map which she kept in the car, she discovered that a small city named Yorktown was less than thirty miles away.

"Ned, I have an idea that is where Monsieur Pappier went! It's too late for a printing shop to be open, but he may be staying at a hotel. Let's follow him!"

"All right, if you want to, Nancy. But it's a long drive. Won't the folks at home be worried about you?"

"I'll telephone Mrs Chantrey and tell her our plans," Nancy declared. "We'll stop at the first drug store."

When Nancy called the Chantrey cottage, she was unable to reach her friends. She assumed the group had not returned from the concert and decided to drive on and call from Yorktown.

Forty-five minutes later, she and Ned entered the Yorktown Hotel. While Nancy tried again without success to get an answer at the Chantrey cottage, Ned checked the register. Monsieur Pappier had not registered for a room there that night, nor had the clerk seen anyone remotely answering his description.

"Perhaps he went to another hotel," Nancy said uncertainly.

The young people went the rounds, but learned nothing. Nancy had known the trip might end in failure, but even so, she was bitterly disappointed. At the last place, the Koven House, she placed another telephone call. Again there was no answer from the Chantrey home.

"Surely they're back by now!" she thought nervously· "I hope nothing has happened to them!"

Ned tried to allay Nancy's fears by telling her that a strong wind which had sprung up might mean there had been a bad storm at Candleton. The wind could have affected the telephone wires.

"It's going to storm here," he added. "Shall we wait until it's over or get started?"

Nancy thought they should leave. But as they walked towards the entrance, she stopped to look into the restaurant where there was dancing, and spoke to the hat-check girl. When she joined Ned her eyes were sparkling like stars.

"Ned, I just learned something interesting! A Spanish Señora who sells cosmetics has been in here tonight! She hasn't registered, but she said she was coming back."

"We're not trailing a Spanish woman, Nancy."

"We may be after tonight! Oh, I'll bet Madame and Monsieur change their nationality whenever the police get warm on their trail!"

"The police!" exclaimed Ned. "That's the ticket! Let's dump this in their laps, and start for home before that storm breaks."

A stop was made at the Yorktown Police Head-quarters where the night inspector assured the couple a close watch would be kept for both Monsieur Pappier and the mysterious Señora.

Trees were cracking in the wind as Nancy and Ned drove out of town. Before they had travelled five miles, the storm broke in all its fury. Lightning zig-zagged across an inky sky and deafening claps of thunder seemed to shake the lonely, seldom-travelled road.

The wiper was chugging back and forth, but water pelted down so fast the glass could not be cleared. It was impossible to see three yards ahead.

"We'll have an accident if we keep on in this!" the young man declared as the car swerved and nearly went off the pavement. "What do you say we pull up somewhere and wait until the worst is over?"

Ned removed his foot from the accelerator pedal and started to ease on the brakes. Before he could do so, the couple heard the screech of rubber tyres directly behind them.

The next instant their car was rammed violently from the rear!

· 18 · *Danger in the Storm*

NANCY and Ned were thrown against the windscreen. The car skidded, but fortunately did not overturn. Though stunned by the force of the impact, Ned put on the brake and switched off the ignition.

They heard loud exclamations and screams from the car which had caused the accident.

"Are you hurt, Nancy?" Ned asked anxiously.

"Just shaken up," she managed to say jerkily. "How about the people in the other car?"

Ned craned his neck to peer out of the rear window into the pelting rain. He saw that the driver was slumped over the steering wheel. But someone was climbing over from the back seat to push the man aside and take his place.

"They're going to get away!" Ned exclaimed. "Hey, you!"

He tried to open his door, but it had jammed. The

new driver of the other car backed quickly down the road. Before Nancy and Ned could get out, he had turned into a side road and sped off.

"Let it go," said Nancy weakly.

"We'll have to let it go," agreed Ned in disgust, looking at the rear of his automobile.

A tyre was flat, and the mudguard was jammed tightly against it.

"Those men fled from here so that they wouldn't have to pay damages!" he exclaimed. "We didn't even see who they were. Now we're stranded!"

"Maybe not." Far down the road Nancy saw the headlights of an approaching vehicle. "Maybe we can get a lift."

Ned signalled the approaching truck and the driver pulled up.

"Havin' trouble?" he called cheerily.

"Yes!" replied Ned with emphasis. "My car's out of commission. Any chance of a lift into Candleton?"

The trucker, who was hauling a load of chickens to a city market many miles away, assured the young people it would not be out of his way to drop them off at Candleton. In fact, he insisted upon driving them directly to Mrs Chantrey's house.

"Glad to have done it," he said, as they bade him good-bye. "I don't have to be at market until six o'clock."

Lights blazed in the cottage, telling Nancy that her long absence had worried the members of the household, and that they could not sleep. Mrs Chantrey, George and Bess greeted the couple joyfully, asking what had happened.

"We'll tell you everything," Nancy promised, sinking into the nearest chair. "But first, is anything the matter with the telephone? I called and called."

Investigation revealed that the instrument was out of order for outgoing as well as incoming calls. Nancy and Ned related what had occurred at Yorktown. Then, at Mrs Chantrey's insistence, Ned accepted an invitation to stay overnight, and everyone wearily went off to his or her room for a much-needed sleep.

It was nearly noon the next day when Nancy was wakened by her friends, who told her that Mr Drew had arrived from New York. Dressing quickly, she ran downstairs to greet him with an affectionate kiss.

"Did you find out anything about those swindlers?" she asked eagerly.

"No," he reported in disgust. "Our leads were worthless. Not only Harry Tyrox, but all the rest of his gang have disappeared completely. But I hate to give Mrs Chantrey this bad news."

"Why not wait for a few days?" Nancy suggested.

She told her father about all that had happened since he had left, including the two times she thought she had seen Tyrox; her experience in Yorktown; the new clue which she hoped might lead to the arrest of the perfume seller; and what she had learned from the people in Candleton who had bought *Mon Coeur* stock.

Although Mr Drew was shocked to hear about the number of investors in town, he was delighted at his daughter's progress with the case. The lawyer decided to motor to Yorktown himself to learn what luck the police were having in tracing the mysterious Señora, and set off in Nancy's car. Ned had gone off a short while before to see about having his damaged automobile repaired.

Left to themselves, Bess and George insisted Nancy relax and go for a swim. They rented a motorboat and went to Whistling Oyster Cave. After a delightful hour in the water, the three friends lay on their backs in the soft, warm sand. Suddenly Nancy sat bolt upright.

"Why didn't I think of that before!" she exclaimed, springing to her feet. "It may explain everything!"

"You might try doing a little explaining yourself," drawled George, tossing a pebble into the water. "What's rolling round now in that clever little mind of yours?"

"The best idea I've had in a week! Girls, you must go to Bald Head Cave with me at once!"

"Not inside," objected Bess. "As a matter of fact, I don't even want to go close to the entrance."

"It's low tide now—just starting to change," Nancy declared excitedly. "I want to make an experiment. You take me round the point of the cliff and drop me off. Then hurry back to the cave."

"And if we do drop you off, what are your plans?" asked George.

"That depends upon what I find among the rocks on the ocean side. But please hurry. I want you to drop me off and get back to the cave entrance as soon as possible."

"Your scheme sounds risky to me," Bess complained. "Anything else you have in mind?"

"Yes, you're to watch the mouth of the cave closely. If the bell tolls or water rushes out, note the exact time, then return to the beach for me."

"You've certainly worked out your little blueprint in minute detail," George said. "Just what do you expect to discover among those rocks on the ocean side?"

"I'll tell you later, after I'm sure I'm right," Nancy grinned. Catching a hand of each of her friends, she pulled them towards the boat. "Come on! The tide is starting to come in, and there's no time to lose."

The boat presently slipped round the point into the ocean. As Nancy started to dive out, George seized her by the wrist.

"Maybe you'd better not do this. At least, not unless you tell us exactly what you have in mind."

"All right. I have a theory that as the tide comes in on the ocean side of the cliff, it may rush through a tunnel in the rocks and gush out of the cave entrance."

"You mean before the tide is very high on the White Cap Bay side?" George asked, turning the matter over in her mind.

"That's my idea. You recall that when we heard the bell toll, the tide had not turned in the bay."

"There may be something to it, Nancy. But what about the tolling bell?"

"I'll know more after I've made my investigation, George. Now will you let me go?"

"All right," her chum agreed, "but do be careful. We'll keep watch at the cave entrance and return here for you."

Diving out of the boat, Nancy swam off and easily reached the shore. As the rocks were sharp, she put on her beach shoes which she had tied round her neck. Up and up she climbed, clinging tightly to precarious holds.

The tide was coming in fast. Waves licked greedily at Nancy's heels, only to fall back in angry froth and foam.

Above Nancy, a fisherman who had been seining with a large net and now was on his way home, saw the girl. He signalled to her, but she was so engrossed searching for a narrow opening in the rocks that she did not see him.

"The tunnel must be lower down," she decided and started to descend. "I believe I see the place!"

Nancy slid towards a pile of debris deposited by the

incoming waves. Crossing this, she went over to a definite opening in the rocks. Only then did she hear a shout from above.

Pausing, the girl glanced up at the ledge where the old fisherman was motioning frantically to her. His words sounded like "High tide!" but she did not catch the rest, because the wind was blowing away from her.

Nancy hesitated, then advanced again in her search for an opening amid the rocks.

But before she could move, a net weighted by sinkers was slung over her. The next instant, Nancy was swept from her feet.

Enmeshed in the dripping net, she was swung up towards the top of the cliff!

· 19 ·   *Confidential Information*

FOR several seconds, Nancy swung precariously in the net above the dashing waves. The old fisherman struggled to lift her the remaining few yards to the rocky shelf, but as he puffed and strained she began to fear that he lacked the strength for the task.

"If he drops me now, I'll never get out of this net alive!" she thought in terror. "I'll be dashed on the rocks, or so tangled in these meshes that I won't be able to swim!"

With one last effort, the old fisherman brought the net almost to the shelf. Nancy, forcing an arm up through the opening above her head, clutched at a small tree which had grown from a crack amid the rocks. She had just caught hold of it, when the fisherman lost his grip on the net!

Desperately Nancy grabbed for the tree with her other hand, and got a toe hold among the rocks. The old man pulled her to safety. Both were breathless and so shattered by the narrow escape that for a moment they could not speak. Then the fisherman gasped in apology:

"I thought I could swing you up easylike! You never should have been foolin' around down there! More than one person's been drowned when the tide comes in!"

"But I knew what I was doing," Nancy defended her actions. "I came here searching for an opening in the rocks. I know about the cave with its tolling bell and rushing water. I thought I could find an explanation for them over here."

Nancy explained her belief that strong waves, dashing through a small opening, might be responsible for the rush of water through the big cave.

"Could be," the fisherman agreed, drawing on his pipe. "But I've lived hereabouts for well on sixty years. I've never heard tell of any such hole in the rocks."

"Did you ever see the ghost or hear the bell?" asked Nancy.

"I've never seen the ghost, and don't want to. But I've heard that mournful bell," the old man replied. "Jim Wester, a young fisherman who was caught out in a heavy fog, lost his life. Him and his boat was never found. Folks figure maybe it's his spirit that's come back to prowl in that cave. Leastways, the bell sounds powerful like the one he had on his old dory."

"A boat with a bell on it might be caught somewhere in the cave," Nancy said thoughtfully. "Has no one ever investigated to find out?"

"Folks hereabouts got too much common sense. Anyway, what good would it do for a body to go in there and fetch the bell? Long as it tolls a warning, it keeps a lot o' people out o' trouble."

Nancy talked for a while longer with the fisherman, but soon was convinced he could contribute nothing to a solution of the baffling mystery. Observing George and Bess on their way back, she signalled to them.

"If you're agoin' down to join your friends, I'll show you a safe path on the bay side," the fisherman offered.

He pointed out a well-worn trail which Nancy followed without difficulty. Reaching the beach, she found George and Bess waiting for her a hundred yards from shore. After knotting her shoes about her neck, she plunged in and swam out to the boat.

"What happened at the mouth of the cave?" Nancy demanded as soon as she was in the boat. "Did the bell toll?"

"Exactly on the hour," George replied. "We didn't see the ghost, but the water did rush from the cave the same as before."

"Then I'm sure I'm right," Nancy said excitedly.

Relating her experience and her conversation with the man, Nancy said she thought it possible that an old, wrecked boat with a bell attached might be lodged somewhere deep within the cave.

"You mean when the water comes through, it makes the bell ring?" Bess asked. "But, Nancy, how do you explain the ghost?"

"So far, I can't. The ghost must be a person. But where does he come from and where does he go? Frankly, I can't guess who would have a reason for hiding there or dressing up in white robes. The only way to solve the mystery is by thoroughly investigating the cave."

"Not today!" said Bess emphatically.

Nancy smiled as she turned to start the motor of the boat. "No, I promised Dad and Mrs Chantrey I wouldn't venture in there even at low tide. But that promise certainly hinders me."

"It may save your life, though," declared George. "This is one mystery I feel we should leave unsolved!"

Nancy did not debate the matter. Her silence as the trio returned to Candleton told Bess and George more clearly than words that she had not the slightest intention of abandoning the enigma of the tolling bell cave.

Nancy had no opportunity to discuss the matter with her father that night. On reaching the Chantrey cottage, she learned that he had sent word he planned to remain another day in Yorktown.

"That means he must have run into some interesting clues!" Nancy thought. "Perhaps the police have traced those scoundrels we're after!"

At Nancy's suggestion the three girls spent the evening at the Salsandee Shop, assisting their hostess. While George and Bess helped prepare Dandee Tarts, Nancy waited on table, hoping she might see Amos Hendrick again. But the old man did not dine there that evening.

Among the customers she saw the same dwarf-like stranger who made a practice of carrying food to his wife. He ate rapidly, with a display of very bad table manners. When he finished, he ordered the usual package of food, and departed. Though Nancy questioned several of the waitresses, no one could tell her the man's name nor where he lived.

"I've certainly seen that man somewhere before," she thought. "It wasn't in the theatre, and yet he seems like someone acting a part."

"He reminds me of a brown-skinned elf," one of the waitresses contributed. "Only he has such mean, cruel eyes!"

"An elf!" exclaimed Nancy. "Why, that's it! I mean—" she amended hastily, "—he does have that appearance."

The waitress's words had recalled to Nancy the strange dream she had experienced many days before on the cliff above Bald Head Cave. In a flash she knew that the characters in her dream were not visionary but actual persons! Now she had identified one of the "elves"!

"I didn't walk from the cliff by myself," Nancy reasoned excitedly. "I was carried by two men. But why?"

Realizing that such a theory might sound fantastic to the others, she was careful to say nothing about it, not even to Bess or George. Nevertheless, she determined to learn more about the stranger.

Hoping that he might lunch at the Salsandee Shop, she made a point of working there the next day. The man did not come, but to her delight, Amos Hendrick strolled into the tearoom. As usual he had a startling remark to make before Nancy could speak.

"Well, well, my favourite waitress again!" he greeted her with a chuckle. "You bring a fellow bad luck, though."

"What do you mean, Mr Hendrick?"

"A. H., if you please," he corrected her. "Remember that man I was telling you about who was going to sell me a bell?"

"You mean the one you met on the other side of the bay, a Mr James?"

"I haven't seen him since, and he was going to bring the bell for me to look at," A. H. reported. "Now I'm afraid maybe I'll never see him again, and I believe he has something I've been hunting for all over the country."

"Not the jewelled bell?" Nancy asked excitedly.

"Mr James didn't tell me much, but I have a sneaking suspicion that it might be," Mr Hendrick confided.

Nancy was startled at the information. She instantly concluded that if Mr James were Harry Torox, he had not secured the jewelled bell by honest means. Perhaps he did not even have it, but knew where it was and was trying to get hold of it. This might account for his not contacting A. H. again.

"Unless his reason is because he has left this part of the country permanently," she thought.

Nancy hoped this was not true, and asked the bell collector to let her know the minute he heard from Mr James. Mr Hendrick promised to do this if possible. Then she inquired what kind of a tone the jewelled bell had.

"Oh, a very pleasant musical sound, almost like one in the middle register of a set of chimes."

"Then your lost bell couldn't possibly be the one in Bald Head Cave?"

"Oh no, that one has a deep tolling sound." A. H.'s eyes brightened. "I'd give a lot to get my hands on it just the same," he declared, "but I value my life too much. Can't figure a way to keep from drowning, or you can bet your last dollar I'd be inside that cave this minute!"

"Perhaps I can help you," Nancy said.

While the old man listened with rapt attention, she told him of her theory that the cave was flooded for only a few hours each day, and that the period of danger could be clocked accurately.

"Say! Maybe I'll go there sometime!" the old man exclaimed. "You really think it's safe?"

"I have an idea that if a person doesn't venture into the cave after the tide has started to come in, he won't be bothered with the rushing water. I'll let you know later."

Because Mr Hendrick was so pleased at the information she had given him, he talked more freely as he ate his luncheon. As she served his dessert, he surprised her by saying:

"I've been thinking things over since I've been sitting here. I have a hunch that man James may be mixed up with the thief who has the jewelled bell."

"How?" Nancy asked, trying not to show her eagerness to hear his answer.

"Didn't I tell you I traced it to a son of the original thief? His name is Grumper. He's an ornery little fellow with a misshapen back. Haven't actually seen him, but I've been told he's around here."

"You think Grumper still has the bell after all these years? Wouldn't he have been tempted to sell it, or at least the jewels?"

"Not Grumper. He's a strange sort of fellow, not much concerned with money. They tell me chemistry is his main interest in life. He got into a jam with the chemical company where he worked, and disappeared. I've good reason to think he's skulking round here somewhere."

"How did you learn Grumper had the bell?" Nancy asked curiously.

"From that note found in my father's possessions. You saw only part of the message."

Nancy would have asked many more questions, but just then another customer sat down at a nearby table. A. H. immediately became silent. Soon he left the tearoom, so the girl had no further opportunity to talk with him.

"He certainly didn't tell me all the story," Nancy thought. "I must see him again and learn the rest."

Later that day she and Ned went to the boat dock with the intention of renting a motorboat to do some further exploring at Bald Head Cave. There they learned that Amos Hendrick had rented a boat and had gone alone to Bald Head Cave.

"He may get into trouble there!" Nancy said anxiously. "I'm afraid he took a theory of mine too seriously. I should have warned him not to enter the cave until I've had a chance to prove my idea about the tides. If I should be wrong, he might drown!"

"Then we must go after him, and we've no time to lose!" declared Ned.

With Ned at the wheel of the motorboat, they raced up the bay. Nancy peered nervously ahead, hoping to catch a glimpse of the elderly man. But he was not in sight.

"Oh, Ned, I'm so afraid we may get there too late!" she exclaimed.

· 20 · An Identification

WHEN Nancy and Ned reached Bald Head Cliff in the motorboat, they could not find a trace of A. H. They had no way of knowing whether or not he had ventured into the cave.

"Say, who is that up there on the cliff?" Ned demanded suddenly. He pointed to a short figure on the high rocks, peering intently at them through a telescope. It was not Mr Hendrick as George had thought the time she and her friends had seen a man on the cliff with a telescope.

"He certainly looks familiar!" Nancy remarked. "Why is he watching us, I wonder?"

Her attention was distracted by a flash of white near the cave entrance. Distinctly she saw a ghostly figure retreat into its dark interior. Within a few moments a bell from within the cave started to toll.

"The warning!" Nancy exclaimed. "Oh, what if A. H. is inside!"

Should this be true, it was too late to do anything to save the man. Fearfully, Ned and Nancy watched as water began to boil from the entrance. A box floated clear, but to their intense relief, no body or overturned boat was washed from the cave.

Convinced that A. H. could not have been trapped by the flood waters, Nancy sighed in relief, and suggested that they climb the cliff to question the man with the telescope.

"He may be able to answer a lot of questions about this place," she said.

Accordingly, Ned anchored the boat, and the couple waded ashore. They climbed the rocks, using the path up which Nancy had gone before. But when they reached the top, the man had disappeared. They walked round, but could not find him.

"Show me the place where you went to sleep that time," Ned suggested.

Nancy ran ahead, searching for the exact spot. When she thought she had located it, the girl paused to catch breath. Presently she began to feel a trifle dizzy from her exertion. The blue sky above seemed suddenly misty, as if a film had dropped over her eyes. Vaguely she recalled that the same symptoms had overtaken her the first day she had visited the cliff.

"Ned!" she called in a weak voice. "Ned!"

He ran quickly towards her. One glance at her face told him something was seriously wrong.

"It's probably the climb," he said solicitously. "I'll carry you to the beach and you'll feel okay."

He quickly lifted her up in his arms and worked his way down the steep slope. By the time they reached the beach, Nancy seemed better.

"Why, I don't know what came over me," she apologized, deeply embarrassed. "I've never had spells like this before!"

Ned insisted upon their going home at once so she could rest, but after he had left Mrs Chantrey's, Nancy subjected herself to a severe athletic test. She raced up and down stairs four times without pausing. George and Bess, who entered the cottage unexpectedly, stared at her in amazement.

"I'm not crazy!" laughed Nancy. "I'm only trying to determine if I get fainting or dizzy spells after strenuous exertion."

"You're a star athlete, if you ask me!" retorted George. "Why, you're not even breathing very hard."

"I feel fine! This test certainly proves I'm all right. But there was something weird about the way I nearly fainted while on Bald Head Cliff! Twice while up there I became very drowsy—almost as if I'd been drugged!

Do you suppose some gas could have escaped from crevices in the rocks where I was standing?"

She had noted no unusual odour other than a sweet one like that of the wild flowers on the cliff, and was unable to offer a satisfactory theory for the strange symptoms she had experienced.

Later that afternoon, at Nancy's suggestion, the three girls called upon Mother Mathilda to ask her if she knew anything about the cliff that might throw some light on the girl's experience. To their disappointment the woman could offer no explanation. So far as she knew, no gasses or deadly fumes had ever exuded from crevices in the rocks.

"I'm glad you dropped in," the elderly candlemaker said. "When you were here the other day, I forgot to tell you about Amy Maguire."

"A daughter of the Maguires who lived on the cliff?" Nancy inquired.

"Yes. She was an adopted daughter. Amy was a wild one, and not really a Maguire, although she took the name. As long as Grandpa Maguire was alive she behaved herself pretty well. After his passing, she made her adopted Ma a heap o' trouble, running off to marry a no-good."

"Someone you knew?"

"No, and I never did hear his name, nor what became of the couple. But I know her adopted Ma was heartbroken. And her Pa took it kind of hard, too. They never mixed with other folks after that."

As the girls rose to leave, the old lady timidly inquired if any progress had been made in tracing Monsieur Pappier, the *Mon Coeur* stock swindler.

Nancy assured her that Mr Drew was working on the case. "We have good reason to think both he and

Madame may be caught within the next few days," she added.

"I hope he's sent to jail for at least twenty years! And that she's punished, too! Will I get my money back, do think, or will the scamp have spent it?"

"No one can tell that until they're caught. But let's hope you'll recover part of it, at least."

Nancy's words cheered the old lady. Grateful to the girls for taking so much interest in her troubled affairs, she insisted upon presenting each of them with a dozen delicately perfumed candles.

"I used good perfume this time, and the entire batch turned out perfectly," she declared proudly.

A little later, at the Chantrey cottage, Nancy learned from Juno that during her absence she had received a telephone call from Yorktown. Knowing that it was from her father, she stayed indoors for the next hour, and as she had expected, he telephoned her again.

"Nancy, I've been trying to get you," he began in an excited voice. "How soon can you reach Yorktown?"

"Why, I don't know," she replied. "You have my car, and Ned's is in the garage being fixed."

"Then catch the first train you can," the lawyer instructed. "The police are holding that Señora you eard about. She may be the seller of *Mon Coeur* perm . You're needed to identify her."

"I'll come as fast as I can," Nancy promised.

With the assistance of George and Bess, she packed a few belongings into an overnight bag and consulted time-tables. The only train to Yorktown that evening was a local which stopped at every station.

"I have no choice but to take it," Nancy sighed. "It will be a tiresome trip."

As it developed, the journey was not tiresome, but

proved to be both pleasant and profitable. Soon after the girl had settled herself in a carriage, Bert Hamilton sauntered in.

"Hello," said the young chemist who had analyzed the *Mon Coeur* cosmetics, as he sat down beside her.

During the trip the young people kept each other company. The chemist displayed keen interest when Nancy steered the conversation to her recent experience at Bald Head Cliff. He looked serious when she revealed her theory that her drowsiness might have come from inhaling some strange fumes.

"I could mention several kinds which have no noticeable odour, and others with a sweet odour," Bert said. "But I've never heard of any near White Cap Bay."

The slow train finally reached Yorktown. With reluctance, for she really had enjoyed the long chat, Nancy said good-bye to Bert. Descending from the coach, she looked about for her father. He was not at the station to meet her, so she went directly to Police Headquarters.

As Nancy entered the building, she saw the lawyer talking to the desk sergeant. He turned, and seeing her rushed across the room.

"I'm glad you're here, Nancy!" he exclaimed. "If you're able to identify the prisoner we may crack the case!"

"Where is the woman, Dad?"

"She's in a cell now. But you'll have to select her from a line-up. Think you can do it?"

"I'll try."

"The woman will not be wearing a costume, which may confuse you," Mr Drew warned.

"If I've ever seen the woman before I think I'll

recognize her," Nancy said quietly. "Tell the police I'm ready."

· 21 ·   *A Dust-Covered Bible*

As NANCY, her father and two police officers stood behind a screen, other policemen escorted five women across a small stage which was brilliantly lighted.

All were heavy-set, dark-complexioned and wore street clothing. Blinking under the bright lights, they stared straight ahead.

Nancy gazed at each woman in turn. Then, without the slightest hesitation, she said, "The one in the centre is the perfume seller. She is known to me only as Madame."

"Good!" praised Mr Drew. "That makes the identification positive."

After the prisoner had been led away, he told Nancy that previously he had identified the same woman as the one who had accompanied him in the taxi to Fisher's Cove.

"The woman who drugged you!" Nancy cried.

"I'm convinced of it. We'll place charges against her."

Nancy learned that Madame, who had been posing as the Spanish Señora while in Yorktown, had been caught by the police as she sought to sell *Sweet Chimes* perfume to the proprietor of a beauty parlour. She had denied knowing Mr Drew or having anything to do with the *Mon Coeur* firm.

"She refuses to tell us anything about her confederates," the lawyer added. "Fortunately, a number of names and addresses were found in her wallet when it was searched. The police are checking them now."

As Nancy and her father stepped into the corridor, they came face to face with Madame, who was being escorted to her cell by two policewomen. Seeing the girl, she suddenly halted to glare at her.

"Your meddling did it!" she cried furiously. "You're responsible for me being held here! But just wait until I get free! Just wait!"

Nancy made no reply, and the woman, still muttering threats, was led away.

"Madame speaks English without an accent," Mr Drew observed. "The truth is, she hasn't a drop of foreign blood. She was born in New York City and her name is Mary Smith."

"Monsieur Pappier hasn't been found yet?"

"No, but the police are hard on his trail. They think he's in hiding around here, but I shan't be able to stay in Candleton to await his capture. I must return to my work at River Heights tomorrow. I have an important case up in Federal Court."

"Oh!" murmured Nancy, unable to hide her disappointment. "Then that means we must leave the case entirely to the police?"

"Not unless you've lost interest," he smiled meaningly.

"Oh, Dad! You know how much solving the mystery means to me! I hope those men are still around here."

"I hope so too, Nancy. We are not letting it be known Madame has been caught. In fact, we planted information here and there that she went back to the vicinity of Candleton. I believe she and Harry Tyrox work hand in glove, and he'll trail her there. I'd like to have you stay at Candleton a few days longer to keep in touch with the situation. If anything develops that you think you can't handle alone, I'll try to fly back."

The next morning Mr Drew took the train for River Heights. He had barely left when Nancy asked Bess and George if they would go out to Bald Head Cliff with her again.

"And have you go to sleep on our hands?" George cried. "And maybe be put to sleep ourselves? I should say not!"

"I don't fancy being carried off by a man even if he is an elf!" said Bess. "Anyway, I promised Mrs Chantrey I'd help her unpack a lot of gifts which arrived yesterday."

Nancy finally prevailed upon George to make the trip by promising to go by car and avoiding the cave.

"But I thought you were supposed to stay here to catch a certain Harry Tyrox who is posing as Monsieur Pappier," George reminded her friend.

"I am. Dad and the police set a trap to get him back to Candleton to look up Madame, but they don't think Harry Tyrox will come out of hiding until nightfall. If he's caught, then I'll probably go home and maybe never solve the mystery of the tolling bell, so I want to work on it now."

"How do you expect to accomplish that on top of the cliff?"

"I think there may be some connection between the ghost in the cave and the disappearance of the Maguires. Another thing, I've been giving a lot of thought to that queer dream I had while lying on the cliff. I've decided one of those little elves may have been Grumper—the misshapen man A. H. told me about."

"Oh, Nancy!" scoffed George. "How could he be?"

"A. H. said he thought Grumper was around Candleton. The answer may lie in the Maguires' deserted home," Nancy decided. "Anyway, I'm going to look for a clue there."

Nancy drove to the footpath which led to the cliff, and parked. The girls walked the rest of the way to the deserted house, gazing about in all directions to find out if they had been seen. Apparently, no one was near to observe their actions.

"This place does have a spooky look," George said uneasily, as they went up to the door.

Nancy pushed it open. Everything appeared exactly as she last had seen it. The mouldy, cobwebby food remained on the dining-room table, and the two dust-covered chairs stood at each end.

"I never saw such thick cobwebs in all my life!" George gasped.

A worn Bible on a marble-topped table drew Nancy's attention. Blowing off the dust, she slowly turned the pages until she came to the family birth and death records.

"This is what I hoped to find!" she exclaimed, and pointed to a notation in faded ink. "Amy's marriage is recorded here. Oh!"

"Now what, Nancy?"

"Amy married a man named Ferdinand Slocum! Why, Slocum is the name of the hotel clerk at Fisher's Cove."

"But Slocum is a fairly common name. He may not be the same person."

"True," Nancy acknowledged. "Let's see what else we can find."

The other records were of no interest to Nancy, but she did find among the pages of the Bible a letter which had been written by Amy to her parents. Obviously, it was sent soon after her runaway marriage two years before. In the letter she disrespectfully referred to her mother and father as being far behind the times.

"Maybe I don't love Ferdie," she had written flippantly, "but he's a big hotel man and we'll have a lot of fun together. Ferdie is a man of the world. He's a big business man, not like those boys at Candleton who only think about following the sea. I'll write again after Ferdie and I are settled in our own hotel."

"I'll bet they never were in any better one than the Fisher's Cove Hotel," George guessed after hearing the letter.

"This note explains a number of things that puzzled me," Nancy cried elatedly. "George, our case is closing in!"

"Find anything else of interest?"

"Yes, here's something!" Nancy cried an instant later.

George, however, did not hear her, for she had made an important discovery of her own. "Nancy, look at these cobwebs on the table!" she exclaimed. "They're real enough, but they're not attached to anything!"

"Just put there, you mean?" Nancy bounded across the room to look. "You're right. Someone is using this cottage as a hide-out!"

"But why would anyone go to so much work just to make this place look weird and deserted?" George asked. "We ought to call the police!"

"I agree with you." Nancy spoke quietly as she stooped to pick up a torn sheet of paper from the floor.

"What's that?" her friend asked.

"Mr Hendrick's torn note that was stolen from the Salsandee Shop!" Nancy replied.

George started to cross the room to see the paper for herself. But as she took a step, a masculine voice from directly behind the two girls said coldly:

"Don't make a move, either of you! Put up your hands and march straight ahead!"

· 22 · *Behind the Fish Nets*

AT THE command, Nancy did not turn round. As she slowly raised her hands, she saw in a dusty wall mirror the reflection of the man who had given the terse order.

He was a short, dark-skinned little fellow with an elfin-shaped body. Instantly she recognized him as the man who came frequently to the Salsandee Shop—one of the elves in her dream.

"Step lively and don't try to turn round," he snapped.

Perhaps the man held a weapon, but Nancy could see none in the mirror. She decided to take a chance. Whirling around, she swung her arm directly into his startled face, causing him to lose his balance. As he stumbled backwards, Nancy gave him a push, and over he went! From his hand fell a telescope!

Instantly the two girls followed up their advantage. George plumped herself on the man's chest and held his arms. Nancy searched him but found no weapon.

"You're the one who helped carry me from the cliff!" Nancy accused him. "You and your friend put me to sleep with a gas which oozed up through crevices in the rocks!"

Nancy and George took the precaution to tie the

man's ankles together with the belt from George's dress and then released their hold. They stood him upright against the wall and placed themselves between him and the outside door. Nancy supposed they ought to take the man to the police station, but she was eager to continue her investigation of the old house.

The man muttered some unintelligible words. He leaned against the wall, his hands behind him. Suddenly, from far away and seemingly from deep beneath the house, a gong sounded.

Nancy was startled. A sardonic grin spread over the elfin man's face.

"It was a signal!" Nancy thought instantly, observing his pleased expression. "He must have an accomplice somewhere!"

Recalling how the little man had many times bought food at the Salsandee Shop for his "wife," she reasoned that was who his accomplice might be. Then, too, there was the possibility no wife existed, and that actually the food had been carried to another man.

"Perhaps he carried the food to that second elf I thought I saw in my dream!" she reasoned. "Grumper! If he is anywhere near here, then George and I must be on our guard!"

Nancy was convinced that the man before her had managed to sound the warning gong by pressing a button or pulling a hidden cord. Even at this moment his accomplice might be coming to his aid.

The door behind Nancy creaked on its hinges. Frightened, she turned swiftly. A shadowy figure loomed large in the entrance.

Nancy laughed aloud in relief. It was not Grumper! Instead, Ned Nickerson stood there!

"Hello, Nancy, are you girls safe?" he called

anxiously. "Bess told me you came here. I was afraid—"
He stopped short and stared at the girls' prisoner.
"Who—?"

Briefly Nancy told him what had happened. The
story was cut short by the sullen little man.

"It's a lie! You'll not take me to the police station!"
he shouted. "I won't leave this house!"

The elf-like figure flayed out with his fists, losing his
balance. As he went down, Nancy said:

"Ned, can you take this man to the police station
alone?"

"With one hand!"

"Then go as quickly as you can and come right back.
George and I will stay here."

"Not alone!"

"Yes. I must find out more about this place."

Ned was reluctant to leave the two girls. However,
at their repeated urging, he finally agreed to drive the
prisoner to Candleton and return immediately.

He bound the man's hands behind him, released his
feet, and ordered him to walk to the car. The fellow
had no choice as Ned prodded him from the rear.

George felt somewhat uneasy when she and Nancy
were alone. As Ned and the prisoner disappeared, she
glanced nervously about her.

"That gong—" she whispered to Nancy. "Don't you
think it means someone else is in here? Perhaps in the
basement?"

"Yes, I'm sure it was a signal. He must have pulled a
wall cord to sound a warning."

Nancy began to explore the wall inch by inch. She
found a tiny cord, smaller than her little finger, not far
from where the fish nets hung. As she pulled on it, a
gong sounded far off.

"That's how he did it!" Nancy cried. "But where is the gong? It sounds so muffled—as if it were underground!"

Apparently the house had no basement, for the girls could find no steps or passageway leading downwards. The only outside door seemed to be the one through which they had entered.

Puzzled, Nancy wondered how the elfin man had entered the house. Certainly not through the front door. She recalled the sudden manner in which he had appeared and his terse order, "March straight ahead!"

"Why, to march straight ahead would mean I'd have to walk through a solid wall," she thought. "Or at least through those fish nets!"

Nancy stared speculatively at the wall, almost completely covered with old cord nets to which dried seaweed still clung. On a sudden inspiration she tore away a portion of the covering.

"What are you doing?" George asked curiously.

"Look!"

Nancy had uncovered a door hidden behind the netting. George stared in amazement.

"The house must have a secret room or passageway!" she whispered. "We've found the entrance!"

Cautiously Nancy twisted the knob, making no sound. The door was not locked. Slowly it swung back on its hinges.

"Oh, Nancy!" shivered George, huddling at her elbow. "Someone may be hiding down there! Let's not leave this room until Ned comes back!"

STONE steps led down to a dark, narrow tunnel beneath the old house. Even Nancy hesitated as she thought of the risks involved in venturing below unprotected.

"George," she whispered, "you have my flashlight, don't you?"

"Yes, but it's dangerous for us to go down there!"

"Let me have the flashlight," Nancy replied. "I'll investigate alone. You stay here and watch the outside door."

"Oh, Nancy, please wait until Ned returns!"

"I don't dare. Our prisoner must surely have an accomplice. I'm convinced there's some tie-up between the *Mon Coeur* crowd and the little man we found here. At this very minute one of the gang may be destroying valuable evidence downstairs."

Disregarding George's protests, Nancy took the light and slowly descended the stone steps. Fearfully, the other girl stood guard at the door in the wall.

"Oh, Nancy!" George called nervously. "Do come back!"

"Sh! Everything is all right," her chum insisted.

Nancy moved deeper into the dark passageway until her light could be seen no longer. Above, George waited with growing uneasiness. After twenty minutes had passed, she could not endure the suspense a moment longer.

"Nancy!" she called softly. When there was no answer she shouted her chum's name again.

George became frightened. She was convinced Nancy was lost or in serious trouble somewhere below.

"I'm going down!" she determined.

On the old buffet stood an antique candlestick with a half-burned candle in it. Beside it lay a match. George lighted it, and holding the candle before her, descended the steps.

Reaching the bottom of the stairway, she groped her way along the passage until she glimpsed a closed door a short distance ahead. Just then her light began to flicker violently and suddenly went out. George had no way to relight it.

As she was about to turn back, she suddenly became aware of footsteps. The tread seemed too heavy to be Nancy's!

George flattened herself against the wall just as a figure brushed past her in the dark. A moment later a man was silhouetted in the doorway at the top of the stairs. He went through, closing the door behind him.

Stumbling up the stairway, George tested it. Her worst fears were confirmed. The door was locked! She and Nancy were prisoners underneath the cottage!

Giving way to sheer terror, George kicked and pounded on the door, shouting for release. No one came to free her.

"That man, whoever he is, has probably left the house," she thought. "Oh, why did I ever let Nancy get us into this mess?"

Nancy! George recalled with alarm that she had come below to find her friend. Remembering the other closed door, the girl groped her way to it. At her touch it readily moved inwards. Nevertheless, she hesitated on the threshold, sniffing the air.

George could see nothing, for the room was dark, but she did notice a strange, sweet scent. As she breathed deeply, a dizzy, giddy feeling took possession of her.

"Why, Nancy had these sensations just before she fell asleep on the cliff!" George recalled. "Oh, I'm being drugged!"

With all the strength she could muster, George pulled the door tightly shut. She felt so weak her limbs barely could carry her away. Through sheer will power she stumbled along the passageway and up the stairs. Dropping to the floor, she pressed her face close to the crack under the door and sucked in great gulps of fresh air.

At once George felt better. Her head cleared and she no longer was weak or drowsy. Then, realizing that she had barely escaped being drugged into unconsciousness, a feeling of panic for Nancy's safety came over her.

What had become of her? She surely had disappeared beyond the closed door because there was no other place to go. At this moment she might be lying unconscious in the dark, sweet-scented room!

"I'll have to do something!" George thought desperately. "But what? Oh, why doesn't Ned come?"

Nancy truly was in need of help. After leaving George, she too had reached the closed door, and cautiously opened it.

A dim light burned overhead in the room, revealing a strange sight. Shelves along the walls were filled with bottles, vials, and flasks of coloured liquid. There were quantities of perfume, lipstick, and face powder.

"It's a cosmetic factory!" Nancy thought excitedly. "And yes, they make *Mon Coeur* products!" she added, as her gaze roved to a wooden bench upon which lay scattered samples of both *Mon Coeur* and the newer *Sweet Chimes* labels.

Hanging above the door was a gong. At this instant she became aware of men's voices.

Desperately the girl sought a hiding place. Wooden benches against a wall offered the only possibility. Quickly she crawled underneath one of them.

Barely had Nancy hidden herself than she heard the voices again. To her alarm, the sound seemed to come from behind the very wall where she crouched.

"I'll have to go now," she heard one of the men say, "but you have your orders, Grumper! I arranged for that old fool Amos Hendrick to come to the cave. All you have to do is get his money, and if you're wise you'll keep him there until the tide comes in!"

"That won't be hard to do, Boss," was the reply. "She's due to turn in about twenty minutes."

The voices became more distinct. Lying beneath the bench, Nancy was startled to see that close by, another bench was slowly moving inwards! Evidently it was attached to a secret door which now was being opened by the approaching men.

A rush of cool air struck her face. As she lay motionless, the door behind the bench opened wider and two men with lighted lanterns tramped in. Before the opening closed, Nancy caught a glimpse of stone steps, and guessed that they led directly to the interior of the tolling bell cave.

One of the men was grotesquely misshapen, his head disproportionately large for his little body. Nancy was certain he must be A. H.'s old enemy Grumper. From her position Nancy could not see the other man's face but his stocky figure was like that of Harry Tyrox, alias Monsieur Pappier!

Nancy listened eagerly as the men conversed in low tones. Just then, from outside the room, her own name was shouted in a loud voice.

"Nancy! Nancy! Where are you?" It was George, searching for her friend in the dark passageway.

The two men heard the cry.

"Get to work, Grumper!" the dark-haired one ordered in a whisper. "We have visitors!"

The misshapen fellow pulled a can of blue powder from one of the wall shelves, and with a little water he quickly mixed it into a solution. Dividing the liquid equally into two containers, he jammed one of them into a tiny niche in the stone ceiling and left the other standing uncovered on the floor.

"Now I'll take care of Amos Hendrick!" he muttered.

Slipping noiselessly through the bench door, he closed it behind him. The man with the lantern extinguished the overhead light. Nancy heard him tiptoe towards the other door. There was no further sound, but she was sure he had gone out.

"I must follow him and help George," she thought vaguely. "He may harm her!"

Despite the need for haste, Nancy could not seem to hurry. As she crawled from beneath the bench, a sweet-smelling scent began to fill the room. She became lightheaded.

"The drug!" she thought in panic. "Unless I get out of here quickly, I'll never make it."

Nancy pulled herself to a standing position, but she could not walk. Her feet seemed to weigh a ton.

She knew she never could reach the passageway. Her only hope of escape was through the door behind the adjoining bench. Could she make it?

Using all her strength, she tugged at the bench. It

would not move. Feeling so dizzy that she scarcely knew what she was doing, she made a last desperate attempt to force the door.

"Oh, please open!" she whispered. "Please!"

·24· *Trapped in the Cave*

THE DOOR from the fume-filled room suddenly moved outwards. Nancy staggered through and closed the opening behind her. Then she collapsed on the stone steps.

It was several minutes before her head cleared enough for her to think.

Her flashlight had fallen from her hand. After groping about in the darkness, Nancy recovered it and focused its rays upon the dial of her wrist watch.

"Only ten minutes until the tide is due to turn!" she thought in panic. "Where is Grumper? If he carries out his orders, Amos Hendrick will surely drown!"

Without considering her own safety, Nancy started down the steep descent to the cave. When halfway down, she heard the tinkle of a beautiful, sweet-toned bell. Switching off the flashlight, she paused. Some distance below her she saw a faint flash of brilliant light.

Making no sound, Nancy swiftly descended the stairs. The passageway veered slightly to the right. As she rounded the corner, she saw a white-hooded figure seated on the ledge inside the cave. The "ghost" was swinging a small bell which gave forth a sweet, musical sound.

"Just as I thought!" Nancy told herself as she hugged

the damp wall to keep from being seen. "This is the interior of the tolling bell cave! And that ghost can be only one person—Grumper!"

As the bell swung back and forth, it gave off flashes of iridescent fire. Only priceless diamonds of great size could provide such a rainbow of colours!

"The jewelled bell!" Nancy thought excitedly.

She had not the slightest doubt that she was gazing at the stolen Hendrick heirloom. Even as she watched, the ghost raised his hood to peer eagerly towards the mouth of the cave.

Suddenly she heard the splash of oars and realized that someone in a boat had ventured deep into the cavern.

At intervals, Grumper tinkled the bell. When the boat came quite close, he suddenly stripped off his disguise and flung it aside. Then, still clutching the precious bell, he crept forward.

Nancy now could see that the man in the boat was Amos Hendrick. Presently he tied up the boat and stepped on to the rocky ledge. As he did so he saw the half-crouched figure.

"Grumper!" he exclaimed. "So we meet at last!"

"Yes, you trailed me to Candleton, but it will do you no good!" cackled the deformed little man.

"You're wrong about that," retorted A. H. His eyes gleamed as he looked at the bell. "I won't haggle over price, but you'll sell it or go to jail!"

Grumper chuckled evilly. "That's impossible. You couldn't get the police if you tried. It's too late! The hour of doom is upon you! The bell is mine, and I also will taste revenge for what your father did to my father!"

"Grumper, you're crazy! My family always treated

your father with more respect and consideration than was his due. The truth is, he robbed my grandfather while working in his forge! Give me the bell or I'll take it from you. I have three times your strength."

"You may seize the bell, but you'll drown! Any moment now the waters from the ocean will rush through this cave!"

Nancy, who knew the threat was no idle one, called frantically from the stairway:

"A. H.! A. H.! It's true! The tide will turn any minute! We must all get out of the cave before it's too late!"

The old man looked at the girl as if she were a ghost. "Nancy Drew!" he exclaimed. "How did you get here?"

"Never mind! We're all in danger!"

"Oh, yes, the tide!" exclaimed A. H. in a startled voice. "I forgot!"

"Come with me up these stairs!" the girl ordered. Grumper snarled at the girl and barred the man's path.

"You'll have to fight me to get past here!" he chortled. "Anyway, it's too late! I can hear the water now!"

Hopping about gleefully, the crazed fellow swung the bell. A. H. pushed him aside and dashed for the steps. Grumper indulged in a fit of sardonic laughter.

"The waters of the cave will swirl to the very top of the stairs!" he chuckled. "You can't open the door without a key, because it locks itself from this side."

"Quick, you fool!" Hendrick cried. "Give us the key!"

"I threw it away! We'll all die here together!"

Nancy and A. H. were frantic. Although it seemed utterly useless, they started up the stairway. Grumper trailed them, gloating over his enemy's predicament.

"Why don't you try to save yourself?" Nancy asked, hoping that the crazed fellow might know of some other way out of the cave. "Your boss didn't ask you to give up your own life."

"That guy who calls himself Monsieur Pappier, and Mr James, and half a dozen other names? He'll be my boss no longer." Grumper laughed mirthlessly. "His real name is Harry Tyrox, and he's a trickster and a cheat. Why, he even tried to steal my jewelled bell and sell it to A. H. When I found him out, he bargained with me to share the money I'd get for it. But I've outwitted him! I'll take the bell with me to the bottom of the sea!"

"So that's what upset you?" Nancy asked soothingly. "You thought Monsieur intended to take the bell? Just lead us out of this trap and we'll have the police put that man behind bars."

' It's no use," Grumper replied in a calmer voice. "I have no key. Even if I could open the door, we could not escape through the fume-filled laboratory."

"Then we really are trapped here?" Nancy asked, losing heart for the first time.

"Yes, we're trapped. You're young and pretty. I'm sorry you have to go, too. I tried to warn you. When you first came to the cave I tried to frighten you away, and later I tried to scare you with sleeping fumes. But you would not leave me alone, so you must suffer the consequences."

The trio had reached the head of the stairs. Below, in the cavern, they heard a faint, gurgling sound.

"The water is starting through," Grumper said. "In a moment now the water will come in with a rush!"

In desperation, Nancy pounded on the heavy door, trying to smash a panel. She succeeded only in bruising her fists.

"Help! Help!" she called weakly.

Then Nancy was certain that her mind was playing a cruel trick on her. From behind the door she fancied she heard footsteps and a muffled voice!

·25· *The Secret Revealed*

AGAIN Nancy pounded on the heavy door. Again she heard the muffled voice on the other side, but she could not make out the words. Maybe the person was asking where the door was.

"The bench!" she cried. "Pull on the bench!"

An eternity elapsed, and the water was coming very close. Then slowly the door was pushed open. The dreaded fumes rushed out, but Nancy, holding her breath, staggered forward. Behind her came A. H. Grumper, paralyzed with fear, cowered on the step.

Nancy caught a glimpse of their rescuer, a young man in a gas mask which protected him from the fumes. She was amazed to recognise Ned!

"Water coming!" she gasped. "Man still below!"

"Go on!" he shouted to Nancy.

Nancy assisted Amos Hendrick to the passageway where the air was comparatively fresh. Ned darted down the stairway. After much prodding he was able to get Grumper to the door. Barely in time to prevent the laboratory from being flooded, Ned pushed the bench door shut.

Then he turned to Grumper. The man had collapsed on the floor, a victim of the very fumes he had concocted!

Ned picked him up in a fireman's carry. As he staggered into the cottage with his burden, he pulled off his gas mask. Nancy's first question was:

"Where's George?"

"She went down to the cave entrance with a trooper," Ned replied. "Nancy, you owe your life to George," he said soberly.

"And to you!" Nancy said.

He waved aside the remark and continued:

"When I delivered your prisoner to State Police Headquarters, I asked one of the troopers to return here with me. We couldn't find anyone inside the cottage. After a while we shouted, and heard George pounding on the secret door behind the fish nets."

"Then she must have trailed me down into this passageway!"

"Yes, she did. George was convinced you were lying unconscious in the fume-filled room. Fortunately, the trooper had a gas mask, a flashlight and other equipment in his car. That's about all there is to tell, except that when I couldn't find you in the laboratory I became desperate. Just as I started upstairs again I heard you pound on the door."

Nancy was too shaken to say much. At this moment George rushed into the cottage wild-eyed. Seeing Nancy, she flung her arms about her friend.

"Oh, you're safe!" she cried. "And I thought—"

Ned turned Grumper over to the State Trooper. "Anyone else downstairs?" he asked.

"No," Nancy spoke up, "but the worst scoundrel of the lot—Harry Tyrox, who also calls himself Monsieur Pappier—escaped," Nancy revealed.

"Just give me a description of him and we'll find the crook," the policeman said confidently. "I'll notify

Headquarters over the short-wave radio in my car."

He was true to his word. Within an hour Harry Tyrox was captured on the road while attempting to flee in a stolen car.

Nancy and her friends had returned to Mrs Chantrey's cottage. A telegram was sent to Mr Drew, telling of the arrests.

"Good work, Nancy," the lawyer replied by wire. "Knew you would not need me to clear up the case."

The next day Nancy and the others were given permission to talk to Grumper and Harry Tyrox. Little by little the entire sordid plot was pieced together.

As Nancy had expected, the confessions of the two men implicated Ferdinand Slocum, the hotel clerk in Fisher's Cove. He, too, was brought in for questioning. At first the man maintained his innocence, but finally admitted his part in the swindle.

"Tyrox and I were friends. He offered me a cut in the perfume business if I would let him use the hotel for some of his shady deals," he confessed to Nancy. "After your father saw Harry in New York, he wired me that Mr Drew was coming to Candleton and something had to be done to delay him at Fisher's Cove. So I told Amy we had to get busy."

"Your wife?"

"Yes."

"Go on with your story."

"I might as well tell it from the beginning. Soon after we were married, my wife Amy mentioned the secret door and passageway leading to the cave. Her foster father had a workshop down there."

"Surely he didn't build the tunnel himself?"

"No, it was there when the Maguires bought the cottage. Old Grandpa Maguire discovered the closed-up entranceway one day when he was repairing the wall, and the secret always was kept in the family.

"The cave originally was used as a hide-out by pirates," Slocum resumed. "The stone carvings are believed to have been their work."

"Tell me about the cosmetic factory," Nancy urged. "Whose idea was that?"

"Harry's. I foolishly told him about the workshop above the cave, and right away he thought he saw a chance to make big money. First, he got the Maguires out by telling them Amy had committed a crime and they would be disgraced when the townspeople heard about it. They packed up and moved away immediately."

"How did Grumper figure in the scheme?"

"Harry knew about him and some crimes he'd committed. He promised Grumper a lot of money if he'd come in with us and work as our chemist. Grumper thought he could use the money to go away some place where no one knew him, so he agreed. But he didn't figure on Amos Hendrick."

"He upset Grumper's plans?" Nancy inquired with a smile.

"He turned them upside down. Grumper was in terror that A. H. would find him and reclaim the stolen jewelled bell."

"How did he learn Mr Hendrick was in Candleton?"

"Through his cousin Franz, who served as a lookout at the cliff. Whenever people came near the cave, he sounded the gong and Grumper, hearing it in the laboratory, rushed down and tried to scare them away with his ghost act."

"And the rush of water had nothing to do with his appearances," said Nancy. "Nor the tolling bell?"

"No, but they sometimes happened close together," Slocum replied. "Whenever Franz spied someone on the cliff, he would run down to the laboratory and have Grumper send up sleeping fumes through that opening in the rocks."

"Then Franz was the second little elf I thought I saw in my dream!" Nancy exclaimed. "He was the one who came so frequently to the Salsandee Shop and carried away food. I suppose he also stole the note A. H. lost there!"

"That's right. Franz knew A. H. by sight and happened to see him drop the note in the tearoom. Later he took it from the drawer where somebody had put it. Before Franz could show it to Grumper, Tyrox got hold of it and then the cat was out of the bag. He tried to get the bell, but Grumper wouldn't let him have it. Tyrox was afraid of him because he could put people to sleep with his drugs."

"You haven't told me how my father was drugged," Nancy reminded the prisoner.

"When your father told Harry he intended to prosecute, he knew we had to do something quick. Harry followed him to the airport, then telephoned Madame that Mr Drew was on his way here. We were ordered to see that he conveniently disappeared for a few weeks. Grumper made up a vial of sleeping fumes, and gave it to Madame. She managed to get into a taxi with your father, and just before leaving it, broke the bottle and dropped the liquid on the lapel of his coat."

"Then how did my father reach Fisher's Cove Hotel?"

"The driver of the cab had been paid by our men and knew what to do. He took your father there. I registered him under another name, and then kept an eye on him."

"It was Madame, I suppose, disguised as a chambermaid, who moved my father from his room."

"Right. Every so often when he was getting better, she gave him another dose and put him to sleep. My wife Amy threw a wrench into the machinery by warning you not to come to the hotel. She was afraid I was getting in too deep, and wanted to spike the entire plan."

"Your wife was far wiser than you, Mr Slocum."

"I wish now I had listened to her," the hotel clerk said miserably. "My wife works in a beauty parlour. The day you came for your father she borrowed a wig from there, dressed as an old lady, and looked for you in the lobby."

"Then she was the one who dropped the note into my lap!"

"That's right."

"Were you in a car that bumped into an automobile I was in one rainy night?"

"Yes, Tyrox and Amy were with me. I was driving and rammed your car by accident. Tyrox recognized you and was afraid we'd be identified. So he grabbed the wheel and drove off."

Nancy and her friends were happy when they learned that Harry Tyrox, alias Monsieur Pappier, still possessed a portion of the money he had fleeced from innocent victims. Mrs Chantrey, Mother Mathilda, and the others who had bought the worthless stock recovered a good proportion of what they had put into it.

"What will become of Amy?" George speculated, as the girls were sitting on the Chantrey veranda one day discussing the case. "Her husband will be sentenced to prison, and she'll be left alone."

"The Maguires are taking her back," Nancy replied. "Mother Mathilda told me the news today. They're all moving to the cottage in a few days—which reminds me, we should go there this minute!"

"But why?" asked Bess in surprise. "All the crooks have been caught."

"True, but the mystery of the cave is only half solved. Mr Hendrick recovered the jewelled bell from Grumper. But we know it wasn't his bell that frightened people away from the place. Another bell must be somewhere in the cave. I intend to find out now." Nancy sprang to her feet. "Anyone going with me?"

"How about me?" inquired a voice from the driveway.

Turning quickly, the girls saw Ned Nickerson approaching the porch. It was his last day in Candleton, and Bess and George generously declined an invitation to ride with the couple to the Maguire home.

"Why this trip to the cottage?" Ned inquired, as he and Nancy sped along the road. "Anything special in mind?"

"I want to clear away the mouldy food and artificial cobwebs Tyrox and his men left there. The Maquires would be shocked. Then, there's something else."

"What?"

"The bell."

At the deserted cottage, the two spent half an hour cleaning away the debris. Then Nancy looked at her watch.

"The tide won't be coming in for nearly two hours. We'll have time to make a complete investigation of the cave."

"I thought that would be on the schedule," the young man chuckled. "Well, I came prepared! I have a gasoline lantern in the car, and it gives off a brilliant light. We'll really be able to see what's down there."

Equipped with the lantern, the two descended into the passageway. They took the precaution of placing a block of wood in the secret door.

"We don't want to get locked in the way George was," Ned stated. "Even if all those crooks have been captured, this place is still dangerous."

The cosmetic factory bore only a faint trace of fumes. Passing quickly through it, Nancy and Ned descended the stone steps into the cave. With the tide out, it was possible to walk on the ledge to the entrance.

But Nancy turned the other way, and asked the youth to focus the light in that direction. Almost at once she found the gaping hole through which the water rushed. To Ned's astonishment, she reached her arm far back into the gap.

"What are you looking for?" he demanded.

Nancy did not answer, but a moment later she asked his help to draw forth a rusty, corroded bell. As it swung slowly, a doleful tolling echoed in the cave.

"The warning bell!" Ned exclaimed. "How did you know it was hidden back there?"

"I didn't, but I got to thinking about the story of the pirates and the loot they hid here."

"Yes, but the bell never rang until recently," Ned protested. "How can you explain that?"

"My guess is that at the time the pirates hid their loot in this cave the opening was very small and only a little water trickled through when the tide changed. Perhaps they placed the bell where it would be tapped lightly when water struck it, and they'd know the tide had changed. But as the years went on, the rushing waters carved a deeper hole, and more and more water poured into the cave. And just recently the violent action of the water caused the bell to toll loud enough to be heard outside the cave."

"That bell must be very old," Ned commented. "Maybe it has been in this cave since Revolutionary War times."

"I'm sure of it, Ned." Nancy peered at the trademark, then excitedly she said, "This is a Paul Revere bell! Just what A. H. is looking for!"

"Wouldn't you like to keep it? Mr Hendrick already has his jewelled beauty, thanks to you. This could be your own trophy—a souvenir of your successful solution of the mystery of the tolling bell."

"I should like to keep it," Nancy admitted. "A. H. said yesterday he wanted to reward me for recovering the jewelled bell, so perhaps he won't mind my having this one."

"No one could dispute your claim but the pirates," Ned laughed, as he assisted Nancy up the stairway. "And they're not likely to cause you any trouble after all these years!"

"It must have been very exciting in the old days," Nancy said wistfully. "How I wish I could have been here when the cave was a pirates' hide-out."

"They'd have elected you their leader!" chuckled Ned. "You *are* a little pirate, you know!"

"Why, Ned!"

"You're a *Mon Coeur* stealer yourself. I know some people who would like to carry you off!"

Nancy opened the door into the Maguire cottage. Laughing, she said teasingly:

"Why, Ned! If anyone should carry me away, how could I solve more mysteries?"

"Mysteries!" he exclaimed, turning out the lantern. "Haven't you had enough of them?"

Nancy was sure she never would have. Already she was longing for another, and it was to come in the form of *The Clue of the Black Keys*.

"Anyway," said Ned, "there's one mystery I know never will be solved."

"What is it, Ned?"

"Why you always change the subject when I try to talk to you about something that isn't a bit mysterious!"

Nancy merely smiled sweetly, and walked out into the sunshine.

CAPTAIN ARMADA

has a whole shipload of exciting books for you

Armadas are chosen by children all over the world. They're designed to fit your pocket, and your pocket money too – and they make terrific presents for friends. They're colourful, exciting, and there are hundreds of titles to choose from – thrilling mysteries, spooky ghost stories, hilarious joke books, brain-teasing quizzes and puzzles, fascinating hobby books, stories about ponies and schools – and many, many more. Armada has something for everyone.

Book Tokens

Give them
the pleasure of choosing
Book Tokens can be bought
and exchanged at most
bookshops.

Armada